THE HABIT

AN EROTIC ADVENTURE

VICTORIA RUSH

VOLUME 9

JADE'S EROTIC ADVENTURES - BOOK 9

COPYRIGHT

The Habit © 2018 Victoria Rush

Cover Design © 2018 PhotoMaras

All Rights Reserved

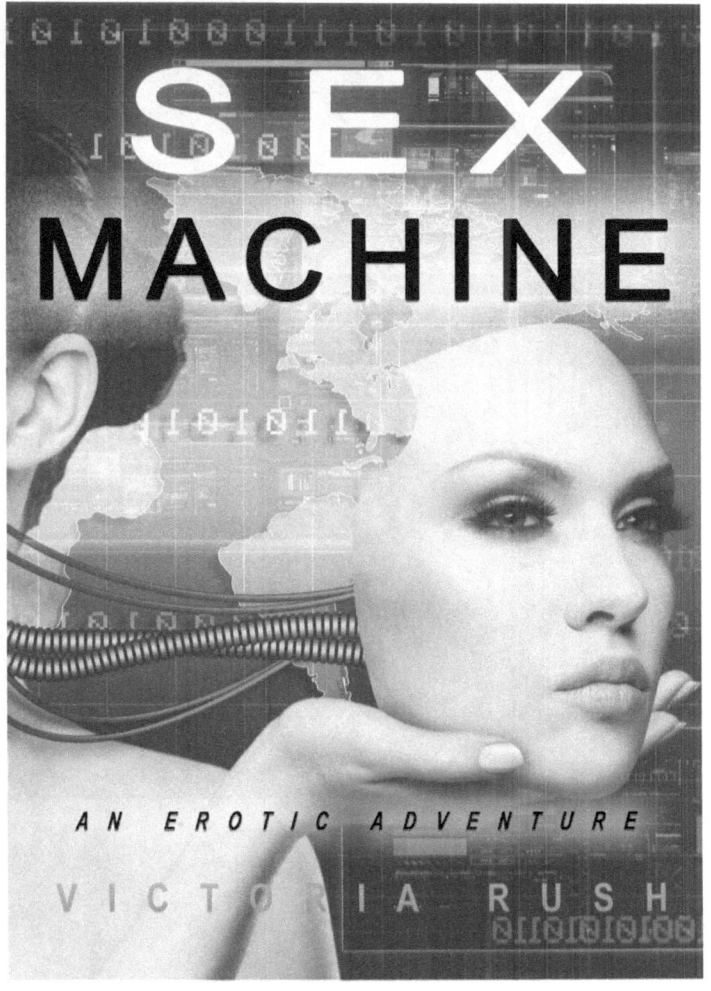

Artificial intelligence never felt so real...

THE
PERSONAL
TRAINER

AN EROTIC ADVENTURE

VICTORIA RUSH

Feeling the burn never felt so good...

Jade's
EROTIC
ADVENTURES

B O O K S   1 - 5

VICTORIA RUSH

Books 1 -5 in the bestselling series - 60% off

THE *Dinner* PARTY

AN EROTIC ADVENTURE

VICTORIA RUSH

Everyone's an exhibitionist in disguise...

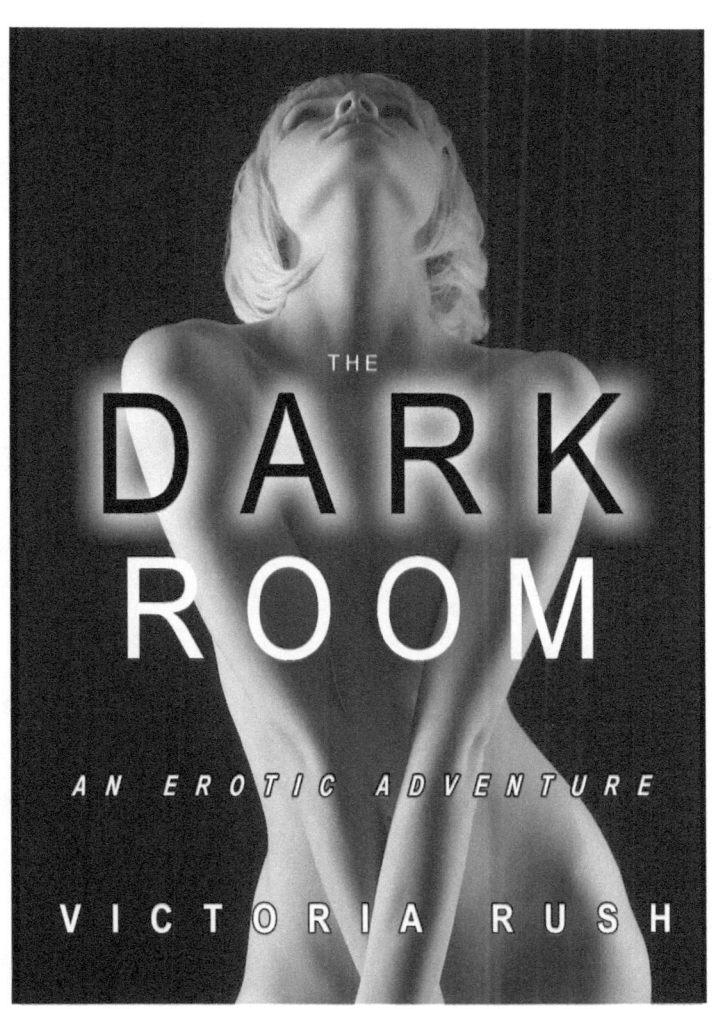

THE DARK ROOM

AN EROTIC ADVENTURE

VICTORIA RUSH

Everything's sexier in the dark...

For the uninhibited...

1

STACKED

I never particularly enjoyed going to the library. Beyond the hassle of dealing with crosstown traffic to get there, it always seemed such a chore to find what I was looking for. Whether I was searching through the card catalogue, the microfilm reels, or even asking the librarian, everything moved at a snail's pace. Having to search through the stacks, access the hard copy, then flip through all the pages to pinpoint my reference material—it all seemed so archaic.

Searching online was so much more efficient. From the comfort of my home office, I could tap in a few search words and within a couple of clicks, get exactly what I wanted. Unfortunately, today, I had no choice but to do it the old-school way. I needed to reference some old newspaper ads to get some ideas for a design project I was working on, and only the library went as far back as I needed.

At least I could count on a relatively quiet environment to do my research. Normally, there were few distractions to get in the way of completing the task at hand. People seemed to respect the rules of public decorum in a library more than other public places like the movie theater or a restaurant. Freed from trilling cell phones and loud side chatter, everybody went about their personal business quietly and politely.

But, today, as I walked toward the microfiche department, something unusual caught my attention. A nun in full regalia stood at the reference desk talking with the librarian. There was something about her manner of dress that seemed out of place among the casual jeans and shorts that other library patrons wore. Her black and white hooded frock stood in sharp contrast to the colorful and largely bare-skinned wardrobe of the other customers.

Like many other bystanders, I caught myself slowing down to stare at her. I saw a few people whispering and snickering amongst themselves as they pointed at her, and I began to feel sorry for the woman. Why should we judge her any differently, I thought, for quietly practicing her faith? There was something admirable about anyone in today's age who could so thoroughly dispense with the material and ego trappings of the modern world.

I was about to continue on my way minding my own business, when the nun turned around. She was much younger than I expected, perhaps in her early twenties, and absolutely stunning. The only part of her that I could see was the front of her face from her chin to her eyebrows. The rest of her head was covered in a white balaclava and hood that draped past her shoulders. She wasn't wearing any makeup, which only seemed to magnify her beauty.

Her pretty face was highlighted with plump rosebud lips, high cheekbones, and soft brown eyebrows. But the feature that stood out most prominently was her eyes. Her irises had an arresting—almost haunting—azure blue color, glimmering like glacial pools surrounded by the snow white hood encircling her head. She could have been a super-model, and for all I knew, maybe she was. How someone that stunning could turn her back on all the temptations and opportunity that would have fallen into her lap, was a mystery to me.

Now I was even more intrigued by this stranger, and as much as I wanted to respect her privacy, I simply couldn't take my eyes off her. The librarian handed her a piece of paper and as the nun headed in the direction of the stacks, I followed a safe distance behind. Her billowing robe covered her body almost to the floor, but I could tell from the tight cinch of her belt around her waist that she had a slender figure under her heavy clothes.

As she walked toward the stacks, I tried to discern the shape and contour of her body, but her heavy vestments wouldn't betray what secrets lay beneath. But this only added to her allure. It was what I *couldn't* see that made her even sexier. I began to undress her with my eyes, imagining a model-perfect figure to match her face, and bit my lip trying to stifle my rising passion. As my panties began to moisten, I felt ashamed responding to this innocent creature in this way, but I couldn't stop.

Get a hold of yourself, girl, I admonished myself, under my breath.

When she retreated into the narrow space between two tall stacks, I stopped by a chair and placed my hand on the backrest for support. I could hear my breath escalating in excitement and had become weak in the knees. I'd never encountered another person—man or woman—who'd had such a powerful and visceral effect on me. I pulled out the chair and sat down, pretending to look through my purse so as not to be obvious that I'd been following her.

There were some loose textbooks in the middle of the

table, and I grabbed one and opened it, pretending to read. I had no idea what the subject matter was because my focus was blurred trying to watch the nun's movement out of the corner of my eye. My pussy was burning in excitement, and I crossed my legs and rubbed my thighs together, trying to give my aching clit some direct stimulation. If there hadn't been so many people around, I would have torn off my clothes and cum within seconds fingering myself.

The nun stood in front of the stack tracing her finger over the spine of some books, trying to cross-reference the call numbers with the paper the librarian had given her. Her eyebrows pinched together in confusion, and for a moment I considered going over to offer some help. But I wasn't sure I could even talk, let alone make any sense, I was so smitten by her beauty. When she leaned forward to take a closer look at one of the books, I squinted to see if I could catch the protrusion of her bosom. But there was nothing to be revealed. It was almost as if she had multiple layers under her clothes to camouflage any hint of her female form.

Those Catholics sure know how to design a uniform to conceal a woman's shape. But I suppose that's the whole point. To minimize the possibility of any temptation—from within or without.

She was wearing a virtually impenetrable barrier to the outside world. My mind began to wander, wondering what kind of undergarments she might be wearing. Was she wearing a traditional corset or a push-up bra? Granny panties or boy-shorts? Nylons or bare legs? Or maybe nothing at all?

You could get away with just about anything under all that get-up, I thought.

I could feel the wetness beginning to spread in the crotch of my tight jeans, and I squeezed my legs together to pull the inseam harder against my throbbing clit. When the nun kneeled down close to the floor to pull a book from the bottom shelf, I couldn't stop myself.

I wish she were kneeling over my face. Oh, how I could give her a taste of earthly delights.

I began to wonder if she'd ever felt the loving touch of another man or woman. Or if she'd even touched *herself*, for that matter. I didn't know much about a nun's vows, but I knew they had something to do with remaining chaste and renouncing most worldly pleasures. It was hard to imagine having no sexual feelings, but if they kept their bodies covered in this manner, it would certainly minimize temptation. The nun never seemed to look beyond her direct field of interest or make eye contact with anyone other than the person with whom she was transacting. Perhaps she'd been trained this way, because there were plenty of scantily clad attractive young men and women scattered about the room to distract one's attention.

Suddenly, she stood up and placed a book under her arm. Then she walked to the rear section of the stacks and turned to walk down the rear aisle beyond my line of sight. After a few moments, I stood up from my desk and went into an adjacent column of stacks to see if I could trace her movement. I pretended to search for a book but instead looked through the space between the shelves to peer through the stacks. I saw her black robe moving to the far rear corner of the library, where she sat down on a large upholstered reading chair.

I grabbed the largest book I could find then headed in the direction of the nun. Not wanting to appear too obvious, I stopped at another upholstered chair about thirty feet away, turned slightly in her direction. I sat down and crossed my legs, then opened the large book on top of my knee. I laughed at my lame attempt at subterfuge, but at least it afforded a modicum of privacy while enabling me to continue spying on my new obsession.

As I peered over the spine of my book at the nun, I struggled to see what she was reading. I couldn't make out the title beyond the large cross appearing on the front cover.

Jesus—is she reading a version of the Bible? Now I'm definitely going to hell for having lascivious thoughts about a devoted woman while she's praying!

But there was no turning back. I was fascinated by this angelic beauty and couldn't take my eyes off her. As she read her book, I studied her face closely from the side. She had flawless alabaster skin, soft rosy cheeks, and a slender, perfectly-straight nose. Whenever she blinked, I could see her long, full eyelashes fluttering over her iridescent eyes. Her expression rarely changed, but every now and then I'd see the edges of her lips curl upwards in a gentle smile as if taken by a passage of her book.

How I'd love to feel those lips smiling around my love button, I thought, feeling my clit tingling in my tight jeans.

The more I looked at her, the more aroused I became, until it was impossible not to touch myself. Having the advantage of elevated padded armrests flanking me on both sides and a large reference book propped up on my legs, I was concealed in my own little cocoon. As long as I was quiet and careful, I could do just about anything I wanted on my chair and no one would be the wiser.

I looked around the room to ensure no one was watching, then I slowly uncrossed my legs and unzipped the front of my jeans and slid my fingers under my panties. But even with the front unzipped all the way, it was hard to reach far enough down into my tight jeans to reach my clit. My fingers pressed against the tight canvas, making it impossible to provide enough room to move around comfortably.

I braced my left arm on the armrest and lifted my hips up slightly, then shimmied my hips just enough to pull my jeans about one inch away from my opening. Now I finally had a little room to operate. My panties were thoroughly soaked, and as I began to circle my clit with the middle finger of my right hand, I had to clench my jaw to stifle my moans. When I redirected my attention back toward the nun, I caught her looking up at me before quickly peering back down at her book.

Shit! I thought. *Had she caught on to what I was doing? She probably runs into all manner of perverts exposing themselves to her whenever she leaves the safety of her convent.*

I froze with my hand down my pants, wondering what to do. The nun seemed to have refocused her attention on her book. My shifting position had probably distracted her temporarily. She couldn't possibly know what I was doing, walled off the way I was. I looked around the rest of the room to make sure I was clear, then slowly resumed fingering my sopping wet pussy.

As I touched myself, I watched the subtle changes in the nun's expression while she read. Her serious countenance made her appear even more model-like, as if she was posing for a camera.

Did she know I was watching her? Did she sense I was turned on by her? If she had, wouldn't she have excused herself?

Was she enjoying being watched?

As I watched her quietly reading, my mind raced thinking of all the dirty things I wanted to do to her if I could get her out of that habit.

What a funny term for a piece of clothing, I thought. *I suppose it signifies her taking on a new form of habitual life.*

Whatever the garment's etymology, I was rapidly gaining a habit of my own for this sexy girl.

Forgive me, Lord. Forgive me the sins of my flesh.

As I began to feel the pleasure rising within me, my legs began to tremble, and I steadied my book on my thighs to disguise what was happening behind my armrests. As I neared my climax, my mouth unconsciously opened and just as I felt my orgasm take hold of me, the pretty nun looked up at me again. She must have known what I was doing from the tortured look of ecstasy on my face, and I looked away in embarrassment.

But I'd passed the point of no return and could no longer hold back the floodgates. As I jilled my clit furiously under my book, I felt the first wave of pleasure sweep over me. I fought to stifle my moans, gagging on the open air with my mouth wide open. I tried to remain as still as possible as the orgasm washed over me, but with each contraction, my chest heaved spastically in my chair.

The fact that I had to disguise the incredible pleasure radiating throughout my body only magnified its intensity. As I sat shaking uncontrollably in my chair, I thought the contractions would never end. I couldn't look at the nun for fear of betraying what was happening, so I peered straight ahead into the blurred text of my book.

When my contractions finally stopped, I slumped down in my chair and exhaled heavily. In my effort to disguise my orgasm, I hadn't realized that I'd been holding my breath the entire time. I panned the room to make sure no one else had witnessed my silent pleasure, then slowly zipped up the front of my jeans.

As I readied myself to silently slip out of the library, I noticed the nun shifting position in her chair for the first time. She crossed her legs and I saw a sliver of skin appearing under her frock above her shoes.

Was she giving me some kind of signal that she knew what I'd done and that she approved? Surely, she'd be discouraged from revealing any more skin in public beyond the small amount of her face?

After a few moments, I noticed a gentle bobbing of her upper foot over her leg.

Was she just indicating that she was happily engaged in her book? Or was this her way of revealing that she was really happy under her habit?

As I peered over the top of my book and watched her more closely, I noticed that her hips were also squirming in her big armchair.

She's rubbing her thighs together as I was earlier, trying to stimulate her clit!

It was hard to be certain, because she continued staring expressionless straight ahead toward her book, but I noticed her eyelashes were fluttering more rapidly than normal. When her lips suddenly parted a few millimeters, there was no longer any doubt.

She was masturbating herself under her gown in plain view of the entire library! I looked around the room to see if anyone else was paying attention, then looked back at her face. Although she never directly returned my eye contact, the subtle changes of her facial expression and body movements told me everything I needed to know. As she rubbed her thighs together more firmly, her legs began moving more rapidly under her heavy tunic. The bobbing of her foot on her knee steadily picked up pace, and her face began twitching almost imperceptibly.

Suddenly, a deep flush fell over her cheeks and her back pulled away from her chair as the cloth of her habit rippled in shockwaves. She was cumming under her habit, and I was the only one to witness it! I jammed my hand into my panties and came hard again as I plunged my fingers into my soaking snatch. I'd never witnessed anything so sexy in my entire life. As I watched her sitting erect in her chair, spasming from her orgasm, my own pussy clamped down over my fingers in sympathy with her.

Although the pretty nun and I never spoke or made further eye contact that day, something told me this wouldn't be the last I was to see of her.

2

OBSESSION

For the rest of that day, I couldn't shake the pretty nun from my thoughts. It wasn't just her celestial beauty—there was something about her veiled appearance that got me worked up. Now that I knew she had sexual feelings, my mind raced with a million questions.

Was this the first time she'd acted on her impulses? Did she masturbate frequently in the privacy of her own room? Or had she simply gotten turned on watching me play with myself? Did she come to the library often for this express purpose? Was this her only safe outlet for expressing her sexuality? If so, why did she choose to live such a sheltered life, if she harbored such strong earthly desires?

But mostly, I just obsessed about what she *looked* like under all her formal vestments. As soon as I got home, I tore off my clothes and imagined our bodies bending together in every possible position. I imagined sucking her and licking her and fucking her, making her come in every possible way I could conjure. I fantasized about making her moan and scream in ecstasy, as I worshipped every square inch of her gorgeous body.

After I came for about the tenth time that day, I lay in my bed exhausted and naked, thinking about how I might see her again. Searching for her at the local abbey was out of the question. They probably wouldn't even allow me to *talk* with her, and if so, it would only be through the front gate for a limited time. And my chances of running into her else-where in the Chicago area were practically nil. For all I knew, the library may have been the only sanctioned area outside the convent that she was allowed to visit.

My only chance for seeing her again was at the library. I knew that today's encounter might just have been a lucky happenstance, but I hoped that our silent tryst had awoken a primal urge within her that she'd want to revisit. My only hope was that she'd return to the library again soon and that this time we'd have a chance to connect on a more personal level. If so, I had no intention of letting her slip through my fingers again. At the very least, I hoped we could have a coffee together to give me a chance to get to know her a little better. I fell asleep that night imagining her lying beside me, our bodies intertwined, her skin still dewy from making love to me all day long.

The following morning, I headed out early to be at the library for opening time. I didn't want to take any chance that I might miss my blue-eyed nun if she had the same idea as me. If I had to stay there all day every day for a month, I was ready to do whatever it took. I packed my laptop to work on client projects in case she didn't show up, but if she did, I planned to be ready. I wore a mid-thigh skirt and my favorite cream-colored silk blouse, with absolutely nothing on underneath. As I walked up the front steps of the library, feeling the cool morning breeze wafting up against my bare pussy, my nipples hardened, producing two protrusions in my blouse.

If she wants more of this, I thought, *I'll really give her a show today.*

When the library opened, I searched every floor and every corner of the facility, but the nun was nowhere to be found. I hadn't expected to see her right away, so I found an open table near the chair where she'd sat yesterday and flipped open my computer. But as much as I tried to concentrate on my work, I kept glancing over at the vacant chair, thinking about what had happened yesterday.

I glanced around the room to make sure no one could see my computer screen, then I typed in the search phrase *videos of nuns having sex.* I paused before hitting the Enter key, then added the word *lesbian.* I didn't want any men polluting my fantasy. A video titled *Confessions of a Sinful Nun* popped up. I clicked the pause button, then inserted my headphones into the audio jack so I'd be able to listen to the video privately. The video was different from most other pornos, with top-quality cinematography, multiple attractive characters, and a real forty-minute story arc.

This should distract me for a while, I thought.

The video began with the mother superior at a convent informing a young nun that two other nuns had missed communion, asking her to search the surrounding grounds for them. The pretty nun headed out along a trail in the woods, and after a few minutes heard the sound of two women giggling in a sheltered glade. She peered through the branches and saw the two nuns fondling each other under their habits. It didn't take long for them to remove most of their clothing, until they were wearing nothing but white stockings.

As one of the nuns lay on the ground, the other one straddled her face, grinding her bush into the nun's mouth. While she humped the girls face, she turned her body and began fingering the other nun's pussy. Before long, the nun on top began to shake, as her breasts quivered on her chest. "Oh yes!" she said, pulling the other girl's head tighter against her pussy. "Right there!" Just as she came on the other girl's face, the mother superior suddenly walked up behind the pretty nun and asked her if she'd seen anything. The other girls overheard the conversation and quickly scampered away, while the third nun covered for them.

If convent life is anything like this, I thought, *no wonder my blue-eyed nun felt the need to travel so far afield to escape the overprotective clutches of her abbey.*

The video was part of an extended series, and as I watched each clip, I fingered myself quietly under my desk. For over an hour, I took myself to the edge of climax, slowly backing down each time. I wanted to save myself for my *own* special nun if she came back. But when one of the scenes introduced a sister resembling the one I saw yesterday, I couldn't hold back any longer. I was just about to cum when a familiar black and white figure emerged from the stacks about twenty feet away.

It was the same blue-eyed nun from yesterday!

She walked directly past my desk looking straight ahead, carrying another book under her arm. She sat in the same chair as yesterday and opened the book on her lap, then peered up over the binding in my direction. Her eyes widened when she recognized me, then she quickly crossed her legs and directed her attention back to her book. I glanced at the chair I sat in yesterday and was disappointed to see that it was now occupied. But from my vantage point just a little further away, I actually had a more direct view of the nun. And from her seated position directly in front of me, she had a clear view of knees and skirt at crotch level.

This could actually work out better than I expected, I thought.

But as the nun kept her head buried in her book, feigning disinterest, I began to wonder if we'd crossed signals.

Had I frightened her away yesterday with my bold overture? If so, why hadn't she just gotten up and moved to a location where I wouldn't be such a distraction?

When her foot started bobbing again on her knee, her intention became clearer.

What a sly fox. She's signaling her interest in me through her body language.

I closed my computer lid to give her an unobstructed view of my upper body, then unbuttoned two buttons on my blouse to reveal my cleavage. As my breasts pressed firmly against the silk fabric, I could feel my nipples hardening once again. The nun looked up from her book and did a doubletake, before directing her attention back down toward her book.

"Yes," I whispered under my breath. "Did you like that? Give me a little more of your attention, and I'll *really* give you a show."

The nun had her head down, but I could see her long eyelashes fluttering in excitement against her brow. I knew she must have been torn between her vow of celibacy and her desire to engage me more directly.

She just needs a little more incentive, I thought.

I shifted position in my chair and spread my legs two feet apart. A few seconds later, she peered up, and I wobbled my knees under the table to redirect her focus. When her eyes dipped under my desk, they widened in shock when she saw my bare pussy exposed under my skirt. This time, she didn't look away.

As I spread my knees further apart, she stared straight into the junction of my thighs. I reached under the table with my right hand and hiked my skirt up a few more inches. She now had a clear, unobstructed view of my bare, glistening pussy. She froze for a moment, staring between my legs, then peered down again into her book, as a flush fell over her cheeks.

I smiled, knowing how conflicted she must have been between her pact with God and the tug of raging hormones racing through her system. There was something about the frustration she was experiencing that made this even more of a turn on. I looked around the room to make sure no one else was looking, then I placed my fingers over my clit and began to circle it slowly.

If she looks up again, I'll make it impossible for her to turn away this time.

I squeaked my chair, and within a few seconds, the nun's eyelashes lifted above her book again. When she saw my hand between my legs, her leg straightened over her knee and her book wobbled on her lap. As I placed my hand over my vulva and began to rub it over my slit, I could feel my juices spilling out of my pussy, coating my thighs and ass. The feeling emanating from between my legs was sublime, magnified all the more knowing my pretty nun was getting just as wet as me under her heavy habit.

As I began to feel my passion rising, my mouth opened unconsciously, and seeing the look of unadorned pleasure on my face, the nun's lips parted also. Recognizing that we'd made sustained eye contact for the first time, I felt an electric charge go through me, and I pressed my fingers tighter against my snatch. I could have come at any moment, but I wanted to savor this for as long as I could.

When her eyes dipped back under my table, I slipped my middle fingers into my opening and began to fuck myself as my two outer fingers slid up and down the inside of my thighs. I wanted to bring my other hand under the table to massage my clit directly, but it was too dangerous. It would have been far too suspicious for any onlookers to see a woman squirming in her library chair with two hands pumping under the table.

Instead, I pressed the palm of my hand against my mound and shimmied my hand up and down over my button while I pressed my two fingers as deep as I could into my hole. The nun was now bouncing her eyes up and down between my face, my bouncing tits, and my cavitating legs under the table. Her foot began bobbing more rapidly on her knee and I could see the front of her frock rising and falling as she breathed heavily.

For the first time, I could make out the bulge of her breasts under her gown, and although they were heavily concealed by all the layers of fabric, I could tell she had a plump set of tits. As I fantasized about sucking on them, I increased the pace of my finger-fucking and spread my legs wider, until they were almost a full one hundred and eighty degrees apart.

As my orgasm began rising within me, my mouth gaped open and I nodded, indicating that I was about to cum, and the nun did the same. Whether she was feeling the same sensations under her robe, or was simply mirroring my expression in sympathy with me, I wasn't sure. When my climax finally poured over me, I thrust my hand hard against my mound and clamped down over my fingers.

As the pretty nun watched the look of ecstasy wash over my face, I pressed back against my chair and sat shaking in a spastic seizure for a full thirty seconds. When my contractions finally abated, I sat up in my chair with my fingers still embedded in my pussy, savoring the heightened sensitivity inside my warm cavern.

When I finally regained my senses, I realized that I'd been so lost in my own pleasure that I'd temporarily lost focus on what the nun was doing. I wasn't sure if she'd managed to rub one out herself, or if she had just been concentrating on enjoying my show. But when she uncrossed her legs and spread her knees apart, her plan soon became apparent. A few moments later, her right hand disappeared from the edge of her book and I noticed some movement under her gown in the area between her legs as the textbook in her lap begin to shake.

Clever girl! It looked like she'd cut a hole in the side of her frock so she could have direct access to her private areas.

The movement under her gown began to take on a familiar and steady pattern as she began to squirm in her seat. Our eyes met once again, and her lips parted as her chest began to rise and fall more rapidly.

Fuck! I thought. *She's actually going to let me watch her come this time!*

I pushed my fingers harder into my pussy and began shimmying my palm against my clit again. But this time, I paced myself so I could cum with her. As her movements under her robe increased in intensity, I sped up my movements in kind. We were staring directly into each other's eyes now, and I could tell she was getting close.

When she nodded her head to me signaling that she was about to cum, I couldn't stop myself from moaning as my second climax took hold of me. The nun's thighs pulled together as she hunched forward in obvious climax, and I gushed all over my hand as the contractions inside my pussy sprayed my love juices all over my thighs and ass. I clenched my face trying to stifle my moans, but a few pitiful whimpers escaped. At this point, I didn't even care if anybody noticed what I was doing. I was on my own special wavelength with the pretty nun across the aisle, and for now at least, we were the only two people in the room.

After a few seconds, the nun's body relaxed and she lay back against her chair. The book resting on her lap popped up as she pulled her hand from between her legs, then she smiled at me softly and closed her eyes, laying her head on the backrest. I looked around the room to make sure no one else had witnessed our silent affair, then I pulled my sopping fingers out of my cunny and cleaned them with some wet wipes in my purse.

There was no way I was going to leave the library alone today without at least talking to the pretty nun. When she stood up from her chair ten minutes later and walked toward the stacks to return her library book, I quickly collected my belongings and followed her. A dribble of lubrication run down the inside of my thigh as my pussy pulsed in excitement, knowing I was about to have my first real contact with the blue-eyed beauty.

3

SISTERS

W hen I entered the row where I saw the nun go to return her book, she was bending forward squinting at the call numbers on the spines of the shelved books. I stepped forward and tilted my head down slightly, smiling at her.

"You know you don't actually have to reshelve library books when you're finished with them," I said.

She stood up, flushing in her cheeks when she recognized me.

"Oh—yes," she said, in a soft voice. "I just figured the librarians can use all the help they can get. There's so few of them looking after such a big place."

My heart raced as I listened to her talk. She was even more beautiful up close than I imagined. She had flawless unblemished skin, and her azure-blue eyes penetrated me like a laser, deep into my soul. Completing the angelic imagery, her melodious voice reminded me of the virtual assistant on my phone, lulling me with its lilt.

I glanced at some of the book titles on the shelf in front of her and the category banner at the side of the stack.

"You're a fan of historical fiction?" I said, trying to break the tension.

The nun glanced at the marker, then smiled as she turned her book cover around for me to see.

"Not usually. Normally I stick to scripture and other Christian themes. But the title of this one intrigued me."

"*Jesus and the Riddle of the Dead Sea Scrolls*," I said, reading the title of her book. "That certainly sounds like it qualifies."

"I think its miscategorized. It's really more of a critique of the Bible, suggesting that the Dead Sea Scrolls offer a somewhat different explanation for the events surrounding the time of Jesus."

"Sounds interesting," I nodded. "What was your impression of the book?"

"I...kind of lost interest after the first few pages," the nun hesitated, looking away. "I guess it didn't exactly fit in with my world view."

She looked at the laptop bag slung around my shoulder and peered back at me with her piercing eyes.

"How about you? What were you reading today?"

"Oh," I said, momentarily caught off guard. "I wasn't actually reading anything specific today. I just like to come here every now and then to find a quiet place to work on some...personal projects."

The nun turned to face me directly, holding her book over her breast like a schoolgirl.

"What kind of work do you do?"

"Freelance graphic design mostly. Book covers, ad copy, corporate logos, that sort of thing." I looked at the pretty nun's smock and frowned. "Pretty superficial stuff compared to your life's work, I would imagine."

"You mean *this*?" she chuckled, pinching her gown and pulling it away from her body a few inches. "I think most people imagine the life of a nun to be one of the most boring vocations possible for a young woman."

"I wouldn't exactly choose that word. I imagine you have plenty of spiritual and emotional stimulation in your chosen field."

The nun nodded gently and sighed.

"Yes, there's plenty of that. Perhaps not as much intellectual stimulation as in your field, though. That's part of the reason I like to come to the library. There are lots of other —*perspectives*—to be found here."

Now I was the one who could feel a blush spreading over my cheeks. I paused, wondering how I could steal a few more private moments with her.

"I'd love to learn more about your life. It's all so mysterious. Do you have time for a coffee? You could enlighten me on spiritual matters, and I could regale you with all the fascinating logos I've worked on."

The nun chuckled, then paused to contemplate my offer.

"I'm not sure you'll find the life of a cloistered nun terribly interesting. I'm sure you have a far more fascinating life. Coffee might be breaking the rules though. I'll be happy to share some fruit juice with you."

I smiled, beginning to realize how pure and unspoiled she was.

"Fruit juice it is. I know a quiet spot not too far from here."

I extended my right hand slowly.

"I'm Jade."

The nun extended her hand and clasped mine softly in hers. My heart thumped in my chest, sending a surge of hormones racing to my pussy.

"Sister Caroline," the nun said.

"Should I address you as Sister, Caroline, or Sister Caroline?" I asked, unsure of the proper protocol.

"Sister is fine."

"Pleasure to meet you, Sister. May I offer you a ride to the coffee shop?"

"Sure. It's got to be more comfortable than the two buses I took to get here."

The pretty nun and I continued making small talk on the way to the coffee shop, with neither one of us broaching the subject of what had happened between the two of us earlier at the library. When we got to the coffeehouse, I ordered two fruit juices and we found a quiet corner of the shop near the fireplace with two upholstered chairs.

"This is a cozy little spot," the nun said. She closed her eyes and took a deep breath through her nostrils. "And the smell is divine."

"I thought you didn't like coffee?"

"This aroma is bringing back the memories. After taking my vows, I gave up a *lot* of little pleasures I'd almost forgotten."

We paused for a long moment smiling at one another, then the nun took a sip of her juice.

"Do you mind my asking what kind of vows you've taken?" I asked. "I'm ashamed to admit that all I know about nuns is what I saw in the movie The Sound of Music."

"We could do worse than that in terms of public perception," the nun chuckled. "That was another one of my favorite things from my previous life, to steal a phrase. I always admired Julie Andrews. I think her depiction of a nun's life is partially what drew me to it."

My eyes crinkled, recognizing a common bond. I was rapidly developing more than just sexual feelings for Sister Caroline.

"You know you look a little bit like her," I said. "The same piercing blue eyes, soft pretty features..."

"You're far too kind, Jade. But to answer your question, we take three separate vows for poverty, chastity, and obedience."

"Obedience in terms of adhering to scripture?"

"Actually, the obedience part pertains to our promising to follow the rules of the abbey and the guidance of our abbess."

"Abbess?"

Sister Caroline chuckled.

"That's mother superior, to our Sounds of Music fans."

"And the poverty part? Is that why you can't drink coffee?"

"That wouldn't be breaking the rules, per se. But we're expected to follow a life of austerity once we enter the abbey. The menu at the abbey is kind of bland, but you get used to it pretty quickly."

I paused, unsure how to broach the delicate third subject.

"And the chastity part? Was that something that you had trouble adjusting to also?"

"At first, no. We actually go through a ceremony where we're literally betrothed to Jesus. Once the temptations are removed in the sheltered confines of the abbey, you soon learn to not think about the temptations of the flesh any longer."

"And when you *leave* the abbey?" I said, finally addressing the elephant in the room. "How do you manage the temptations then?"

"I was doing fine," she said. "Until I saw you."

I paused, looking into the nun's eyes with a pained look on my face.

"Sister..."

"I think perhaps you should call me Caroline. It feels a little strange under the circumstances you calling me sister."

"I agree," I said. "Caroline. I like that name. It's soft and pretty—like you."

"I was thinking the same about you, Jade. It's been hard for me to take my eyes off you. It wasn't just because..."

I leaned forward and placed my palm over Caroline's hand resting on her armchair.

"I'm sorry about being so forward," I said. "I couldn't resist. From the moment I first saw you, my body seems to have a mind of its own whenever I'm around you. And then when I saw you reacting to me the way you did—"

"Was it that obvious?" Caroline said.

"Not to anyone else in the library."

"I hope not. Otherwise, my abbey's switchboard will be flooded with calls from outraged Christians."

"You were very...*proper*," I chuckled. "I'm quite sure I was the only one who noticed that you were enjoying more than just your book in your chair."

"Not nearly as much as *you*," Caroline said, her cheeks flushing a deep shade of crimson. "It was a lot more —*obvious*—how much pleasure you were experiencing on the other side of the room."

Hearing Caroline acknowledge our sexual connection for the first time suddenly sent a flood of juices pouring out of my pussy. I crossed my legs, feeling the moisture coating the inside of my thighs.

"You have that—*effect* on me," I said. " I think I could have just as easily—*enjoyed myself*—just watching you. I barely even needed to touch myself."

Caroline smiled at me warmly, as I noticed her bosom begin to rise and fall in silent excitement.

"I'm glad you did though. You're beautiful—everywhere. When I first caught you squirming in your chair yesterday, it was like a different power overtook my body."

I squeezed my thighs together, pinching my clit between my legs.

"While you revisited another one of those earthly pleasures you'd almost forgotten?"

"Yes," Caroline said. "And not just once. I've revisited those pleasures several times since yesterday. You're a difficult image to shake from one's memory, Jade."

As I crossed my legs trying to contain my rising passion, I felt the juices pouring out of my opening, dribbling down the crack of my ass.

"So what do we do now?" I asked. "Keep meeting for clandestine rendezvous at our local public library? Sooner or later, someone's going to catch on to us."

"I think you're right," Caroline nodded. "We're both taking unnecessary risks."

I looked around the coffee shop and noticed many people suddenly turning away. It was apparent that the pretty nun in her black habit had become the center of everyone's attention.

"Why don't we go somewhere where there aren't so many prying eyes? I can make us some more fresh juice at my place. That is—if you don't need to get back to the abbey right away..."

"What time is it?" Caroline asked. "I don't have a watch."

I pulled my phone out of my purse and tapped the screen to wake it up.

"Ten fifteen."

"It's still early," she said. "I might not be missed until the afternoon communion..."

For the entire duration of the twenty-minute drive back to my place, Caroline and I didn't say a word to each other, the sexual tension was so thick between us in the car. As she looked out her passenger window watching the passing scenery, I squeezed my thighs together, trying to keep my throbbing pussy from completely soaking the underside of my skirt.

When we got to my house, I opened the front door and invited her in. She looked around my living room and nodded approvingly.

"You have a lovely home," she said. "Tasteful and understated, just I expected."

"I wouldn't have thought you'd expect anything *understated* about me after today," I laughed. "Come to the kitchen and let me see if I can fix you up something more to your liking."

I led Caroline to my open kitchen and offered her a bar stool at the large central island.

"What do you feel like?" I asked. "Water, juice—or maybe something a little stronger? I don't suppose you're allowed to partake in certain other types of spirits?"

"We do occasionally partake in communal wine," Caroline chuckled, "so long as it's been properly consecrated first. Hopefully I won't be struck down for drinking something other than the blood of Christ, this one time."

"White wine it is then," I said, pulling a bottle of chardonnay from my fridge. "We don't need any more judging eyes upon us today."

I placed two wine glasses on the counter and filled the goblets halfway, then sat down beside Caroline.

"To rekindling forgotten memories," I said, holding my glass in the air.

Caroline tapped her goblet gently against mine, then took a small sip from the glass.

"There's been one other thing I've been meaning to ask you," I said, peering up at her white headdress. "Why is your hood white? Don't most nuns wear a black veil?"

"You're not the only one who's asked me that," she said. "Nuns normally go through a period of testing when they first enter the religious order, called a postulancy. For the first couple of years, we wear a white veil, signifying that we're still novitiates, or novices. Once we pass this initial test, if the nun and the abbess agree that the monastic life is what they desire, we take our final vows and receive the traditional all-black habit."

"So you're still—*testing* the waters, then?"

"I suppose so. I'm getting pretty close to the end of my postulancy period. My mother superior will be expecting me to take my final vows soon..."

"Do you feel ready?"

Caroline paused for a long moment with a pained look on her face.

"I thought I was. Until I met you. Then suddenly, my thoughts were no longer so pure..."

I set my glass down on the counter and stared into Caroline's eyes, imagining how conflicted she must have felt at this moment. We paused for many long seconds peering at one another, then she leaned her face toward me unconsciously. I quickly closed the distance and placed my lips against hers gently. As she closed her eyes, she pressed her mouth harder against mine.

I swiveled my stool until I was facing her directly, then I brought my right knee forward, parting her legs. As Caroline's mouth opened, I felt her cool breath on my face. I pushed my tongue gently into her, tasting the sweet vestige of wine on her lips. Within seconds, we were holding each other in a passionate embrace, pressing our bodies tightly together over the bar stools.

"Jade," Caroline panted, pulling away momentarily.

I looked into her eyes, trying to divine her intentions.

"Caroline," I said. "Do you feel ready?" I repeated.

She peered through glistening eyes at me and paused for only a moment.

"Yes."

Then she leaned forward and closed her lips around mine.

4

UNCLOAKED

Caroline and I kissed awkwardly on the bar stools for a few moments, then I pulled away and suggested we go upstairs where we could be more comfortable. As I led her by the hand through the hall, I felt an electric charge running through my body knowing I'd soon see her disrobed. But when we got to my bedroom, I paused looking at her habit, unsure where to start.

"I feel a bit uncomfortable touching your gown," I said. "Somehow, it just feels—*blasphemous*. I don't know how..."

Caroline smiled softly at me, then reached her hands up behind her veil.

"I can see how it might seem a bit daunting," she said. "Let me show you how I take off my armor."

She turned around and reached under the pleated fold behind her hood, then removed a hidden safety pin holding the two sides together, closing the pin and placing it in her pocket. Then she flipped up the back of her veil and unclasped another safety pin holding the inner flaps together. Then she turned around and lifted her hood off her head. Underneath, she wore a white cotton headdress covering her ears, neck, and the rest of her head.

I stared at her as she disassembled her wardrobe, mesmerized by the multiple layers of strange regalia. She looked so pure and innocent bound up in her tight white hoodie.

"Is there somewhere I can keep my veil?" she said, holding the white hood in front of her.

"Yes," I said, hanging it delicately over the back of my chair so as not to wrinkle it.

When I returned, she had her hands behind her head, slowly untying some more connections.

"Can I help?" I said, frustrated by the slow pace of her undressing. "Two people might make this go a little faster."

Caroline chuckled then turned around. At the back of her head, I saw two cotton ties holding her headdress together.

"You weren't kidding about the body armor," I chuckled. "They've really got you all tied up in this thing, don't they?"

"It's not as bad as it looks," Caroline said. "It's actually quite comfortable. You get used to it pretty quickly."

I untied the cotton bows at the back of her headdress, then gasped. Her hair was shorn down to short stubs, revealing an almost bald head.

"Are you *sure* you want me to take this off?" Caroline said with her back still turned to me.

"Yes," I said. "More than ever." I looked at the back of her hoodie and saw some more clasps. "What now?"

"Remove the safety pin holding the flap at the back of my neck."

I reached up and found the pin and gently slid it out under the band.

"Good God," I said. "How do you manage to get all these

pins in and out every day without stabbing yourself? Or do you just sleep in this thing?"

"Heavens, no," Caroline said. "We're expected to keep our habits in pristine condition. That would produce far too many wrinkles. I actually sleep in the nude most of the time."

My pussy pulsed at the thought of soon seeing her naked body.

"I'm dying to see you that way. How do we get the rest of this stuff off?"

"There's just one more pin to remove," she said. "At the bottom of my collar, you'll find another one holding the two flaps together."

I found the pin and removed it softly.

"Done."

Caroline turned around and smiled at me.

"Are you sure you're ready for this?" she asked.

"Yes," I said. "I want to see *all* of you."

Caroline reached behind her neck and removed her large oval collar and handed it to me. Then she reached behind her head and pulled her headdress forward off her head. When she showed her bare head for the first time, my eyes widened as big as saucers. Her baldness accentuated her soft features and beauty, reminding me of a young Sinead O'Connor.

"Caroline," I said. "You're stunning."

I leaned forward and kissed her on her lips and she pulled gently away.

"Don't forget about the wrinkling thing. I want to see you naked just as much as you do, but I've got to be presentable when I return to the abbey. Let's get the rest of these clothes off so we don't have to worry about it any longer."

She handed me the headdress and collar and I placed

them flat on my work desk along with the pins. Now she stood before me wearing only her long black robe. The slow reveal was driving me crazy, and I could feel my pussy pulsing between my legs, anticipating what lay beneath.

Caroline threaded her fingers between the two sides of a long sash on the front of her gown, then pulled the strange garb over her head and handed it to me. Divest of the extra garment, I saw a long string of black prayer beads hanging down the side of her gown from her belt.

"This is called the scapular," she said.

"No wonder I couldn't make out your shape under your gown," I said. "How many layers do you have on this thing anyhow?"

"Just one more."

She reached around her back and unbuckled her belt, then handed it to me with the beads attached.

"Now the rosary..."

"Are you sure I won't get struck down by lightning touching this?" I joked.

"Let's hope not. But just to be safe, you might want to handle it by the belt only."

I held the belt out in front of me, being careful not to let the beads touch the ground, then laid it gently on my desk beside the other garments. When I returned, Caroline paused, looking at me unsteadily. I could tell she was a little nervous about revealing any more of her body.

"May I do this part?" I said, seeing the zipper running down the front of her tunic.

"Yes," she said, softly.

I slowly pulled the zipper down from under her chin and noticed that she wasn't wearing a bra.

"No undergarments?" I said, somewhat surprised.

"Not today," she said. "I wanted to feel...sexier. Normally,

I wear an undershirt, bra, panties, and nylons. Something told me I might need to remove my habit a little faster today..."

I paused, realizing she was completely naked under this final layer. I stared into her eyes as I slowly pulled the zipper down. Listening to my heart pounding in my chest, I wasn't sure which one of us was more nervous. When the zipper reached the bottom of its travel, I pulled the upper halves of her tunic apart and peered down at her chest. When I saw her breasts, I gasped.

"Oh, God," I murmured.

Caroline's breasts were full and firm, standing in two perfect circles high on her chest. I reached in and cupped them with my hands and squeezed them gently, stepping forward and kissing her hard on her mouth. I could feel her chest rising and falling as she breathed heavily, blowing a soft breeze through her nostrils onto the sides of my cheeks. When I moved my thumb and forefinger over her nipples, I felt them harden, and she gasped in my mouth. As I rolled them gently between my fingers, she pressed her body firmly against mine.

We kissed for a few more seconds, then I moved my hands around the sides of her back, down toward her buttocks. As I ran my hands over her cheeks, they quivered in my hands and I pulled her toward me more tightly. When our mounds touched, we both let out a moan, and I felt Caroline's muscles contract in my hands as she pressed her mound against me.

"Jade," she panted. "This is all I've been able to think about. I want to make love to you."

She stepped back a couple of feet, then pulled her arms out of her sleeves and dropped her gown to the floor. When I saw her fully naked body for the first time, it took my breath away. She had a slender but shapely hourglass figure, with barely an ounce of fat anywhere on her body. Her whole body was white as fresh snow, except for a light brown triangle of pubic hair between her legs. I reached down and picked up her habit and folded it over the back of my chair, then returned to behold my pretty angel.

I stepped forward and ran my hands down the sides of her body, feeling the curvature of her hips, then I cupped her face in my hands and kissed her softly. Her body was shaking next to me, and as I touched her back, I felt goose-bumps on her skin.

"Are you chilly?" I said.

"Maybe a little," she said. "I'm not used to being out of my habit for this long. Maybe I'm a little nervous too..."

"It's okay," I said. "We can take this slow. Let's get you under the covers where you'll be more comfortable."

I pulled the covers down from the edge of my headboard and gently sat Caroline on the side of my bed. Then I kneeled down on the floor between her legs and untied her black shoes and placed them beside my nightstand. With my face so close to her kitty, I could smell her sex wafting up from between her legs, and I wanted to pull myself into her so badly.

But I lay her down on the bed and pulled the sheets and comforter over her, then stood up. As she lay on my bed looking up at me innocently, I began to unbutton my blouse. Her eyes widened when she saw my full breasts pull away from my shirt, and I quickly pulled my arms out of my sleeves and threw my blouse on the floor.

"I'm not quite as worried about wrinkling as you are."

"Neither am I right now," she said. "Just get out of those clothes and get in here."

I quickly undid my skirt and dropped it to the floor.

Even though Caroline had seen my naked vulva from across the library floor earlier, she was surprised to see my bare mound. Her eyes widened as she took in my body, squirming seductively under the covers.

"Now *you're* the one who looks pure and clean," she said, staring at the bare space between my legs.

I pulled off my shoes, then climbed in under the covers next to her.

"I'm sure I'm nowhere near as pure as you," I said, snuggling close to her. "But speaking of clean, I am feeling a little crusty from all the bodily discharges I produced watching you earlier today. Do you mind if I have a quick shower?"

Caroline wrapped her arms and legs around me and squiggled closer to me under the covers.

"Now?" she said. "You'd leave me to my own devices after teasing me so thoroughly?"

"Well if you don't think you can wait the five minutes it'll take me to clean up, you could always join me in the shower."

I turned around and opened my nightstand drawer.

"Or you could keep yourself amused with these other devices while I'm gone."

Caroline's eyes widened as she took in my collection of sex toys.

"Are those what I think they are?" she said.

"You've never used one?"

"Nothing quite so...elaborate. I've experimented using bottles and sundry pieces of fruit before, but these look a lot more—*sophisticated*."

I looked into Caroline's eyes and smiled a wide grin.

"You're in for a real treat then," I said. "But first, I want to have my *own* way with you before you get too attached to mechanical devices. Come, let's have a quick shower together to get cleaned up. It'll warm you up, too."

I threw the covers back then we scampered into my ensuite washroom, giggling like two little girls. I adjusted the water temperature in my shower until it was nice and warm, then I pulled Caroline under the spray. As the droplets bounced off her bald head and streamed down her face, I pulled her toward me and kissed her hard on her mouth. We rubbed our breasts together under the slippery water, clasping each other's buttocks, grinding our mounds against one another.

Caroline moaned gently, and I began to lower myself slowly down her body. As the water poured over me, I kissed her under her neck, tasting her sweet flesh. When I reached her chest, I paused to give each of her breasts plenty of attention, sucking and flicking her hardened nipples with my tongue, cupping and squeezing her tits between my two hands. The further I moved down her body, the more she moaned and whimpered, her stomach quivering in excitement from my touch.

It was obvious to me that she'd never been touched in this way by another person, and I savored every square inch of her magnificent, unspoiled body. When I got to her bush, I sucked the water droplets off her thatch like dew on the morning grass. Then I knelt down on the tiled floor, gently spread her legs, and kissed her pearl. Caroline gasped, grabbing the back of my head, and pulled me closer toward her.

"I thought you said we were going to get *clean* in here," she panted.

"That's exactly what I'm doing," I said. "I didn't say *how* we were going to get clean. Do you want me to stop?"

"God, no!" she said, pulling my head harder against her crotch.

When I slipped my tongue around her button and began to lather her with my serpent, Caroline threw her head back and moaned loudly.

"Yes, Jade," she whimpered. "Lick me. Lick me clean with your tongue."

Caroline's sexy comments surprised me, emboldening me to go further. I cupped her ass with my left hand and began trilling my fingers against her opening. Caroline bent her knees and tilted her hips, encouraging me to go further.

"Yes—take me," she said. "I want to feel you inside me."

I slipped my middle and forefinger into her cavern, and she pushed her hips down until my hand was buried inside her up to my knuckles. As she began humping her hips against my hand, I sucked her lengthening nub into my mouth.

"Oh God, yes," Caroline panted. "Suck me, Jade. It feels so good."

As her humping action increased in intensity, she pulled my head harder against her pussy. I could tell she was getting close, so I curled my fingers against her G-spot and flicked my tongue more rapidly over her rubbery clit. When I slipped my pinky finger further down her perineum and placed it over her anus, she gasped.

"Yes!" Caroline panted. "Jade, I'm going to—"

Suddenly, she emitted a guttural scream and pushed her muff hard into my face, as I felt her vagina and rosebud pulsing against my fingers. As she came into my mouth, I held her firmly in my hands, savoring her sweet nectar as the water streamed over my face.

"Jade—Jade—Jade!" Caroline panted with each pulse of her pussy. "I'm cumming! Oh—I'm cumming into your sweet mouth!"

It was odd to hear someone screaming in the throes of

ecstasy without using any curse words, which just added to my excitement. As I felt the water streaming down over my ass and mound, my pussy quivered along with Caroline's. When she finally stopped shaking atop of me, I stood up and kissed her passionately, as the water streamed down over our faces.

Caroline wanted to return the favor, but I just wanted to get her back into bed as quickly as possible. I let her run the bar of soap over my body and between my legs, but I made sure to not get too worked up. There was so much more I wanted to do with her when we had the full and free roam of each other's bodies. When we were both thoroughly clean, we stepped out of the shower and toweled each other dry, then we scampered back into my bedroom and dove under the covers.

We kissed and intertwined our legs awkwardly for a few minutes, then I pulled myself away.

"Are you thoroughly warmed up now?" I said, looking into her eyes.

"Yes. You've practically brought me to a boil."

"Good," I said, throwing back the covers. "Because this is going to need a little more space."

Caroline pinched her eyebrows together and began to raise herself up.

"What did you have in mind? It's my turn to—"

I placed my hand on Caroline's chest and gently pushed her back onto the bed.

"It's okay," I said. "This is for *both* of us."

I lifted her knees off the bed then gently pressed her legs forward and apart until her thighs were resting on top of her chest. Then I moved my body forward and pressed my mound against hers.

"Uhnn!" Caroline grunted in surprise when our clits touched.

"Yes, Jade!" she said. "Make love to me."

She lifted her head and peered between her legs. Both of our buttons were hard and erect, protruding like little pencil erasers toward one another. I lowered myself slowly and swayed my hips over hers, watching out nubs bending and flexing in a playful little sword fight.

"Oh God," Caroline panted. "That feels so good! Stroke me, Jade. Rub me...*fuck* me!"

I widened my eyes and gasped at Caroline in mock astonishment.

"You dirty little girl," I said. "I sure hope no one else is listening right now. Otherwise you could be in a lot of trouble."

"So do I," Caroline said. "But right now it hardly matters. Take me. There's only one place I want to go right now."

I lay my body on top of Caroline's and began to grind my pussy into hers as we kissed passionately. For the first time, I felt her tongue press into my mouth, and we sucked and nibbled on each other as our hips gyrated together. I wanted to make this feeling last, but I was already so worked up from making Caroline cum earlier, I could feel my orgasm rising quickly within me.

I grunted into Caroline's mouth as my juices poured out of my cunt, coating her bush and thighs with my lubrication. I could feel myself getting close, and I pulled my face up so I could look at Caroline's face. As my mouth and eyes widened signaling my impending orgasm, Caroline suddenly began panting louder.

"Yes, Jade," she said. "*Cum* for me. I want to watch you cum all over me."

I lifted my body up in one last strain and thrust my pussy hard against hers.

"Caroline!" I screamed. "I'm cumming! I'm cumming in your sweet pussy!"

Caroline's pupils suddenly dilated and she called out my name.

"Fuck, yes!" she screamed with me. "I feel you! I'm cumming with you, Jade! Oh God—it feels so good!"

Suddenly, I felt a hard spray jetting up against my vulva as Caroline squirted her love juices into my opening. Feeling her cum against my pussy was too much. I swung my body around her and clamped our boxes together in a scissor position. I wanted to feel our pussies connected as we were cumming together.

"Uhnn—Caroline," I grunted. "Come in my pussy, baby! Fill me up with your sweet nectar!"

I pulled her leg up toward my chest, grinding our cunts together, feeling my contractions gripping my entire body. We jerked and heaved our bodies together for a full minute, watching the look of tortured ecstasy wash over our faces. When we were completely spent, I collapsed on the bed beside Caroline, panting and sweating. We lay beside one another for a long time, holding and caressing each other, then Caroline finally turned toward me.

"What time is it?" she asked.

My eyes widened and I shook my head.

"Oh no," I said. "You can't..."

"I have to," she said. "The abbess will begin to worry if I'm not back soon."

I looked at Caroline through glistening eyes.

"But I don't want to let you go. I wanted to feel you fall asleep in my arms."

I turned my head toward my nightstand, thinking of how I could entice her to stay a little longer.

"And besides, you haven't even tried any of my toys. I had a few special ones in mind for you. When can you come back?"

"I don't know if I can," Caroline said. "These library excursions were meant to be temporary. I'm supposed to stay within the abbey. That's the whole point of my vows—to abstain from worldly temptations."

"But I thought you hadn't decided yet? Hasn't this changed your thinking at all about continuing on your life of abstinence?"

"It has, but I'm not ready to give it all up just yet. I need a little more time to think—"

"Can I visit you at the abbey at least? I just need to see you. I can't just let you walk out of my life forever."

Caroline looked at me with a pained expression and shook her head.

"It's too dangerous. People will notice there's something different between us—"

I reflected back to the videos of the naked nuns I watched earlier in the day.

"Is there somewhere I could meet you then, where no one would notice? Can you ever leave the grounds temporarily?"

"Not really."

Caroline paused for a long moment.

"But—"

"Tell me," I said. "I'll do anything, as long as I can see you again."

"There might be one way," she said. "But it's very dangerous..."

"What? Tell me!"

"I might be able to sneak you into the abbey for a short time. There's a secret passageway that we're not supposed to know about. A few other novices and I occasionally use it to slip outside to go for a walk. But we'd have to do it at night, and we'd need to have a signal."

I paused for a moment, thinking how I could notify her when I was near.

"How about if I hoot like an owl? There's plenty of those around here. Will you be able to hear it from inside the abbey?"

"I'll keep my window open," Caroline nodded. "But not tonight. The abbess will be watching too closely. Let's do it tomorrow night, just after dusk. Hoot three times in succession, so I know it's you. But be sure to do it convincingly, so it sounds like a real owl. I'll meet you at the south gate at the edge of the forest."

"I'll watch YouTube videos and practice all day," I said. "Will I be able to stay the night? I want to feel you in my arms when I fall asleep."

"Possibly. But you'll have to stay holed up in my room until the following night. Then you'll have to leave. It will be too dangerous for you to stay more than one day."

"I promise," I said, feeling my heart beating again in excitement. " Even one more day with you will feel like a lifetime. I just hope you'll reconsider your vows so we can see each other again. I don't want to lose you."

Caroline turned her body to face me and kissed me softly.

"You're so sweet, Jade. If anything could pull me away from the ascetic life, it's you."

Then she paused as she smiled into my eyes.

"And bring some of your toys. That might help."

5

MOTHER SUPERIOR

The next twenty-four hours seemed like an eternity, as I waited to see Caroline again. All I could think about was her radiant face and her pale, supple skin pressed against my body. I'd gone online and practiced my owl imitation as promised, standing in front of my mirror contorting my face and vocal chords, until I thought I'd gotten the pitch just right. As long as nobody saw me huddled in the surrounding woodland, I was confident I'd be able to pull it off.

An hour before dusk, I collected my belongings and drove north toward the remote address Caroline had given me. When I got to the monastery, there was a long drive leading up a hill, protected by a wrought-iron gate. I parked my car on a side street and tried to find a pedestrian access point, but the entire estate was surrounded by a tall iron fence topped with pointed finials, with locked gates all around.

Caroline had warned me about the barricade, so I removed a heavily padded blanket from my tote bag and flung it atop the spikes. I threw my purse over the fence then awkwardly pulled myself up the front of the fence and swung my legs over the top. I could feel the finials poking through the blanket into my stomach and chest, and swung my legs over the other side and fell onto the manicured lawn on the other side.

"These guys don't fool around," I murmured, feeling like a cat burglar invading a hallowed ground.

I made my way up the hill, trying to stay under the cover of the many mature trees scattered over the estate. When I got to the top of the hill, I saw a tall, steepled church flanked by two four-story block buildings. Caroline told me she was in the west residence, so I moved to that side of the compound and waited about thirty feet behind the rear entrance under a large elm tree. There was no sign of any activity on the grounds, which just added to the spookiness of the scene.

What the hell have I gotten myself into? I thought, looking around the quiet estate. *If anybody sees me, I'll stick out like a sore thumb.*

I'd worn special clothing to not be too conspicuous, and with my long dark pants, black sneakers, and black turtleneck, it just added to the cat burglar mystique. As the light dimmed over the estate, bats began darting over the dark sky and I heard rustling in the branches overhead.

This place is creepy, I thought, wondering if this was an omen of bad things to come.

But as dusk fell, I began to hear the familiar hooting of owls in the surrounding woodland, and as I listened to their calls I prepared to alert Caroline. At precisely nine-fifteen, I let out my signal.

"Hoo—hoo—hoo," I called out in my best falsetto.

Within seconds, a nearby owl returned my call.

"Hoo—hoo—hoo," I repeated.

Almost immediately, the owl hooted back.

If I can trick a real owl, I thought, *hopefully I can blend in with the rest of the local fauna.*

I waited five minutes, watching the back door to Caroline's building, but there was no sign of movement.

Had her abbess suspected something different about Caroline when she returned to the abbey and was keeping a closer eye on her? What if she can't get away?

I repeated my owl signal two more times, then I saw the back door swing open a few inches and Caroline stuck her head out, motioning for me to come in. I looked around to make sure the way was clear, then I scampered toward the door and jumped inside. Caroline and I kissed for a moment, then she pulled away with wide eyes.

"Jeesh—" she said, "do you think you could have made more of a racket out there? You've probably woken up the entire western wing!"

"It wasn't just me," I protested. "Apparently, there was another amorous owl out there competing for my affections. We had quite a little conversation going on for a while there."

Caroline giggled, then pulled a folded habit from under her cape and handed it to me.

"What do you want me to do with this?" I asked.

"We're going to need to disguise you, in case we run into anyone. It's only three floors and a short walk to my dorm, but I don't want to take any chances."

"Oh my God!" I said. "As if we haven't already broken enough rules. Now you want me to pretend I'm a *nun*?! God will surely strike me down before I get to your room."

"I'm sure he'll understand, under the circumstances," Caroline said. She removed the long tunic component from the pile. "Put this on first. Do you remember how it goes?"

"I've replayed your undressing ceremony in my head only about a hundred times since you left," I chuckled.

I stepped into the toga, then pulled the sleeves over my arms and zipped up the front.

"Good," Caroline said. "Now for the scapular."

She handed me the long flap draped over the front and back of the habit, and I pulled it over my head.

"Now the guimpe..." she said, handing me the large white collar.

She placed it around my neck and fastened it with the safety pin behind my back.

"Almost done," she said, handing me the white head-dress. "Do you remember how to put on the wimple?"

"Of course," I said, placing my face through the hole in the front, then pulling it up under my chin and over my head.

"We won't worry about tying it at the back," Caroline said. "We haven't got far to go. It should hold until you get to my room. Now for the veil."

She lifted a black hood from my hands and placed it over my headdress, fastening it with two velcro tabs on top of my head.

"Why do I get a black one?" I asked.

"You're going to be a fully professed nun for tonight," she said. "You'll attract less attention this way."

"No prayer beads?" I joked.

"Let's not push it," she said. "You're already living on borrowed time as it is."

Caroline paused, as she looked at me approvingly.

"You know, you look quite suitable in a habit. Are you sure you don't want to consider joining our monastery full time? At least we'd have a chance to be together more—"

"I don't think I could manage the chastity part of your vows very well," I kidded.

"What now?" I said, looking up the stairs.

"Follow close behind me," Caroline said. "If we encounter any other sisters along the way, just keep your head down. Hopefully, nobody will recognize that you're an outsider."

"And if I am?"

"Well improvise."

"Is that where the lightning comes in?"

"Quite possibly."

I shook my head as I followed Caroline up the three flights of stairs, then she opened the door leading to her floor's hall and peered through the crack.

"All clear," she said. "Remember—stay close behind me."

I paused, reaching out to grab her arm.

"Shouldn't the more senior nun lead the way? Won't it look unusual for me to be following you?"

"Don't let that uniform go to your head, my lady. Just follow my instructions and we should be fine."

Caroline swung the door open and stepped out into the hall, then began walking down the corridor with her hands embedded under the sides of her gown. I mimicked her movement, holding my purse tightly against my abdomen, walking three feet directly behind. When we were about halfway down the hall, another nun suddenly turned the corner about a hundred feet ahead of us and began walking in our direction.

My heart raced in fear thinking I'd be detected, and I scurried up closer behind Caroline.

"What do we do now?" I whispered. "Surely she'll recognize that I'm not part of the congregation!"

"Just be calm and keep your head down," Caroline said.

I lowered my head, feeling my loose headdress falling down over my eyebrows, and I lifted my hand to push it back. After we'd closed the distance to about fifty feet, the nun stopped and turned to one of the residence doors and nodded gently toward us. Caroline returned the gesture, then the nun entered the room and closed the door behind her. Twenty feet ahead, Caroline stopped outside another door on the opposite side of the hall and quickly pulled it open motioning me inside. I scampered into her room, and after Caroline checked both ends of the hall to be sure no one else was watching, she slipped in and closed the door behind her.

We giggled quietly, then I pressed her body against the door and kissed her passionately on her lips.

"That was a close one," I said. "Do you think the other nun suspected anything?"

"I don't think so, but just to be extra careful we're going to have to be super-quiet as long as you're in my room. The horarium has ended for the day, so we've got the rest of the night to ourselves."

I leaned in toward Caroline and slipped my knee between her legs, pressing my thigh against her crotch as I kissed her. After a few seconds, she stepped away, pinching her eyebrows.

"Wrinkles!" she said.

"You've *got* to be kidding me," I said. "Don't you have an iron? They must provide *some* appliances to make your life easier—"

"We do. But it will just be easier if we get out of these clothes. Besides, I've been dying to see you naked again ever since yesterday."

"You don't have to ask me twice," I said, eager to get out of my religious garb as soon as possible.

We helped each other remove our garments, then Caroline hung and placed everything carefully in her wardrobe closet. When we were both naked, we pressed our bodies together, mashing our breasts and mounds against one another, kissing passionately. I moaned unconsciously from the delirious feeling of holding her close to me again, and Caroline pulled her face away, lifting her finger to her lips.

"Sh!" she said. "Not a peep. This place is like crickets at night. You can hear everything."

"That's easy for *you* to say," I whispered. "I don't know how I'm going to possibly contain myself around you."

"Well then, I guess you'll just have to do *me* first," Caroline smiled. "I've had more practice keeping quiet around here."

She looked at my large purse resting on the floor and widened her eyes.

"Did you bring some of your toys for me to play with?"

"I did," I said, smiling at Caroline mischievously.

I picked up my purse and placed it on her narrow bed, then pulled out a large purple dildo with a V-shaped extension near the base.

"This is one of my favorites. It's called a rabbit vibrator."

I pointed it up and turned the dial at the base of the dildo. The purple shaft began to vibrate and the tip of the dildo began to wobble in circles, as a ring of beads midway along the shaft began to rotate.

"Those don't look like prayer beads," Caroline said.

"No, but I think you might find them divine in an entirely different sense of the word."

Caroline looked at the animated device, widening her eyes.

"Do I put it *inside* me?"

"It works best that way. The oscillating head twists and

turns, providing a heavenly form of stimulation against your G-spot."

"G-spot?"

"That the place inside you where I tickled you with my fingers yesterday."

"Oh yes—I remember that very well. That was the first time you took me over the edge."

Caroline placed her fingers over the strange rubbery protrusions on the side of the dildo. "What do *these* do?"

"Those are the rabbit ears. They provide direct stimulation to your clitoris while the shaft is pumping and churning inside you. The combined effect is really quite something."

"I can see how you were worried I'm might become too attached to these devices." She reached into my bag and pulled out a leather harness with a long red phallus attached to the front. "What about this one?"

"That's what's called a strap-on dildo. It's something I can use to—um—*make love* to you like a man."

"Do women *do* that to each other?" Caroline said, pinching her eyebrows together.

"Some do. It can actually be quite fun, when you're in the right mood."

Caroline glanced in my purse seeing a variety of other sex toys and shook her head.

"Where do we begin? You've brought so many—"

I pushed Caroline gently down on the bed and lay on top of her.

"First, I want to touch and feel you with my *own* body parts," I said. "I've been dreaming about tasting your sweet body for the past twenty-four hours."

I rubbed my tits against Caroline's and ground my pussy into hers, thrusting my tongue into her pliant mouth. As her breathing escalated, I began kissing my way down the front of her body toward her pussy. I played with her breasts for a few minutes, pinching and sucking her nipples, then I drew my tongue over her quivering tummy until I reached her pubic patch. I flapped my face over her soft bush, breathing her fresh scent deep into my nostrils.

The lower I went on her mound, the wetter her patch became until my face rested between her slickly coated thighs. When I placed my tongue over her clit and licked it like a lollypop, Caroline gasped. I looked up between her legs and she tilted her head down toward me.

"*Now* who's being the noisy one?" I said.

As we peered into one another's eyes, I took her jewel into my mouth and began dancing my tongue over her hard shaft. Caroline bit her lip and scrunched her eyes, trying to keep quiet. It was such a turn-on seeing her face contort in private pleasure as I nibbled on her fiery love button. Her mouth opened wider with her rising passion, and I placed my fingers at her opening, preparing to thrust them inside her. But she reached out and placed her hands over mine, stopping me.

"Wait," she panted. "I want to feel you...*fuck* me...if you're going to be inside me. Can we try your strap-on sex toy?"

I lifted my head and smiled at Caroline like a Cheshire Cat.

"I thought you'd never ask," I said.

I quickly got up off the bed and wrapped the leather harness around my hips then rocked my hips in the air, flapping the big phallus sticking out from my mound.

"Is that what a *real* man's penis looks like?" Caroline asked, wide-eyed.

"More or less," I said. "This might be a little larger than

most, and it has a few extra features distinguishing it from a regular cock."

I tapped a button on the side of my belt and the penis suddenly began bouncing and oscillating from side to side. Caroline's eyes grew even larger, and she tilted her hips up toward me.

"Yes, Jade," she purred. "Fuck me with your big man cock. I want to feel you inside me."

My pussy pulsed and I felt a dribble of lubrication run down the inside of thighs. I ran my hand over the slick patch then rubbed it over the top of my phallus, simulating a masturbation effect.

"Mmm," Caroline said. "I think it will feel even better *inside* me. Stop playing with your cock and put it inside me."

Caroline's dirty talk was getting me even more turned on, and I kneeled on the bed between her legs and placed the tip of my artificial cock over her opening. I rubbed it up and down her slit for a few seconds then I pressed the head against her clit. She rocked her hips forward to provide more friction against her love button and moaned softly. I looked into her soft blue eyes then grabbed her hips on both sides and slowly inserted the cock into her cunny.

"Oh, God yes!" Caroline panted. "Fuck me with your big cock, Jade!"

I thrust my pole deep inside Caroline's pussy and began pulling her hips toward me as I fucked her harder. Her tits bounced up and down on her chest with each thrust of my hips, and she began swinging her head from side to side in pleasure.

"It feels so good, Jade!" she said, seemingly no longer concerned about how much noise she was making. "Fuck me harder. Make me cum all over your big cock!"

I could feel the base of the phallus rubbing against my

own clit as I thrust in and out of Caroline, and before long I began to feel the familiar pangs of an orgasm rising within me. I reached to the side of my belt and pressed the vibrator button, suddenly feeling the device throbbing between my legs. I pushed my hips hard against Caroline's vulva, grinding the oscillating phallus against her clit.

"Oh God, Jade!" she panted. "You're going to make me cum! Here it comes—I'm cumming Jade!"

I looked down between her legs and saw her spraying all over my artificial dick as I pumped in and out of her. Feeling her love juices dripping down under my belt into my own pussy soon put me over the edge too.

"Caroline!" I panted, trying my best to keep my voice to a whisper. "Cum on me, sweetie. I feel you. Momma's coming with you!

I thrust my big dildo into Caroline's spasming pussy for a full thirty seconds, then I fell on top of her, kissing her passionately while I continued to pump my cock into her, savoring the slippery wetness between both of our legs. After a few minutes, I pulled out and lay beside her, kissing her face and neck softly.

"That was incredible," Caroline panted, looking into my eyes. "Those toys really *are* addictive, aren't they?"

"They can be. That's why I like to use them in moderation. There's still nothing quite like the natural feeling of skin on skin."

"Mmmm, I agree," Caroline purred. "Speaking of which, I think it's *your* turn for some good old-fashioned skin-on-skin lovemaking. What can I do for you now?"

"Well, now that you mention it, there *was* something I had in mind.."

I removed my harness and placed the strap-on dildo on the corner of the bed, then swung my legs over Caroline's midsection and shimmied my hips up toward her head. When I got to her shoulders, I lifted my legs and placed my knees on opposite sides of her head. I paused for a moment, watching Caroline stare at my dripping wet pussy, then I slowly began to lower myself toward her face.

Just before I touched her lips, we heard a loud rapping noise on Caroline's door.

"Sister Caroline," an older woman's voice said from the other side of the door. "Is everything all right in there? I heard some unusual noises. May I come in?"

"Um—one minute, Mother Margaret," Caroline called back, her eyes wide as saucers.

She raised herself up off the bed and whispered for me to hide in the closet. Then she went to the wardrobe and opened the doors, putting on a terrycloth robe. I quickly picked up my purse and slipped inside, retreating to the far corner behind the hanging frocks. Caroline closed the door quietly behind me, and I peered between the narrow slats with frightened eyes. Caroline lifted her bedcovers and threw the rabbit vibrator and strap-on dildo under the sheets, then straightened her robe before heading to the door. I couldn't see her and the other nun from my vantage point, but I overheard the conversation clearly.

"Good evening, Mother," Caroline said. "Everything is fine. I was just preparing my bed to go down for the night."

There was a long pause, and I looked around Caroline's room to make sure all of my belongings were out of sight. Fortunately, she'd had the presence of mind to hang my clothes in the closet, so for all intents and purposes, it looked like she was alone.

"May I come in for a moment?" Mother Margaret said. "I'd like to inspect your room to ensure everything is in order."

"Of course. But I don't think you'll find anything out of place. You know how neat and fastidious I am."

"I do," Margaret said. "This won't take long."

I heard some footsteps moving toward the closet, then a nun wearing an all-black habit passed by my door. I crouched lower under the hanging robes and held my breath so as not to be heard. The mother superior looked around Caroline's room and noticed a bump in her covers and bent over to smooth them with her hand. Her eyes widened when she felt a hard object under the covers, and she swung the covers down, revealing the rabbit vibrator.

"What's this?" she asked.

"It's a—" Caroline paused, trying to think of how she could explain the strange object, "...*massager*. It helps loosen up my tight muscles when I get cramps."

"*Really?*" Margaret said, in a condescending tone. "You know most electric devices are banned from use in this abbey. But I might make an exception in this case, depending on your need. Show me how you use it."

Caroline looked at the mother superior in shock as her mouth tipped open.

"It's okay, my child. I merely want to see how it relieves your—*pain*."

Caroline picked up the vibrator by its purple shaft and twisted the control knob on the bottom. The vibrator began whirring and twisting in her hand, and she placed it against the back of her neck, turning her head from side to side, simulating the relaxation of her shoulder muscles.

"That's quite an interesting device," Margaret said. "May I see it for a moment?'

Caroline hesitated, then turned the vibrator off and handed it to her superior.

Margaret held it up in her hands for a moment and

twisted it around in her hands.

"Why is it shaped like a *penis*, I wonder?" she said. She ran her hands over the tip of the phallus. "It appears to be anatomically correct—except for these strange flaps on the side. Where *else* have you been placing this massager to relieve your pain?"

It was obvious to me that Mother Margaret knew full well how the sex toy was designed to be used and that she was enjoying watching Caroline squirm as she tried to explain why she had it in her possession.

"Just my shoulders and back, mostly," Caroline said.

"*Mostly*?" Margaret said. "Show me. Take off your robe and lie down on your bed and show me how you use this thing to stimulate your muscles elsewhere on your body."

Caroline froze as she looked at the mother superior with a terrified look in her eyes.

"Go on, child. I'm *ordering* you. By your vows, you must follow all of my instructions. Let me help you off with your robe."

Mother Margaret stepped behind Caroline's back and pulled her robe off her body, then threw it on the base of the bed.

"Please continue, Caroline," she said. "Lie down on your bed and place that massager where it is designed to go."

Caroline lay down tentatively on the bed and began to rub the dildo over the sides of her body.

"*Lower*, my child. I think it's meant to go lower."

Caroline traced the vibrator down the side of her body until it rested on the side of her hips, then she pushed it into the sides of her buttocks, pretending to massage her hip muscles.

"Now, bring it—*inside*," Margaret instructed. "Between your legs. Place the purple penis between your legs."

Caroline paused for a moment, and the mother superior nodded for her to continue. She pulled the vibrator over her thigh and placed it awkwardly between her legs, rubbing it up and down softly over her slit.

"Yes, my child. Doesn't that feel better than using it to massage your neck or shoulders? Now, I want you to turn it on."

Caroline lifted the dildo above her hips and turned the dial part way. The vibrator began humming softly.

"*All* the way," Mother Margaret said.

Caroline twisted the dial clockwise until it wouldn't go any further. Suddenly, the penis became fully animated, twisting and oscillating noisily in her hand.

"Now place it between your legs, and let's see how pleasurable this massager can really be."

Caroline placed the tip of the humming vibrator at her opening and gasped.

"Does that feel better, Caroline?" Margaret said. "Is this massager relieving your stress in your nether regions?"

"Yes," Caroline panted.

"I think it's designed to massage your *insides* too," Margaret said. "I want to see you insert it into your private area. You've had far too much stress built up these past few months. Let's see if this special massager might relieve you of some of your burden."

Caroline paused for a moment, then inserted the tip of the vibrator into her slit. I could see the oscillating head turning and dancing over her opening, tickling her clit. As her long eyelashes fluttered in obvious pleasure, I couldn't help reaching down between my own legs to play with my own clit. There was something incredibly sexy about watching her masturbate herself while being watched by such an austere authority figure.

"*Deeper*, my child," Margaret said. "Press it deeper inside you. Feel the phallus filling you up, massaging your deepest regions. Relax and enjoy the stimulation of your special massager."

As Caroline inserted the dildo deeper into her pussy, I could see the rabbit ears flapping along the side. When she pressed the ears directly against her clit with the oscillating dildo embedded all the way inside her, she grunted loudly.

"Yes, Caroline," Margaret said. "Doesn't that feel better? Is that relaxing all of your muscles now?"

"Yes, Mother," Caroline panted, beginning to hump her hips, thrusting the vibrator in and out of her. "It feels...very good."

"Continue, my child," Margaret beseeched her. "Continue massaging your inner regions to see if you can relieve *all* of your stress."

"Yes Mother," Caroline panted, beginning to lift her hips off the bed as she hammered the dildo in and out of her.

It was the sexiest thing I may have ever witnessed, and I bit my lip trying to stifle my moans as my juices poured over my hand trilling between my legs.

"Oh Mother," Caroline said. "I can feel it—beginning to —ease my pain. It feels very good."

"Yes, my child. Push it harder up inside you. Make sure it reaches all of your sore muscles."

Caroline lifted her hips high over the bed and pulled the vibrator as far into her as she could, holding the vibrating ears tight against her mound. I could see the wings flapping wildly against her clit as she opened her mouth at the height of ecstasy. Suddenly, she grunted loudly and began shaking her hips uncontrollably.

"Uhnnn!" she grunted. "Oh God, I feel it, Mother!"

"Yes, my child," Margaret said. "Feel his blessing

sweeping over you. You are truly filled with the spirit of Jesus."

Watching Caroline cumming so hard in front of the mother superior unfurled my taps, and I gushed all over my hand as my pussy clamped down over my fingers. It took a superhuman effort to not utter a sound, as I jerked silently in the darkness of the closet.

Caroline held her hips up in the air as she spasmed in a long and sustained orgasm for many seconds. When the wave finally passed, she flopped back on the bed, panting heavily.

"There now," Margaret said. "Doesn't that feel much better? Perhaps we can find a good use for this automated stress-reliever after all."

Margaret kneeled on the bed and took the dildo out of Caroline's pussy and inserted it into her mouth, sucking her juices seductively from the shaft.

"I've been feeling some built-up stress of my *own* lately..."

As she knelt on the base of Caroline's bed and began to lift the front of her habit, she suddenly paused and ran her fingers over the covers. Feeling something else under the covers, she pulled them back all the way, revealing the strap-on dildo.

"What have we here?" she said, looking at Caroline mischievously. "Have you been using these special massagers with some of our other sisters? I think perhaps it's time I reminded you who's *really* in charge around here."

As she began to remove her habit, Caroline glanced toward the closet doors. I wasn't sure if she could see me peering back at her, but I sure as hell could see her and the mother superior vividly. And I was about to get the show of a lifetime from my dark little peephole...

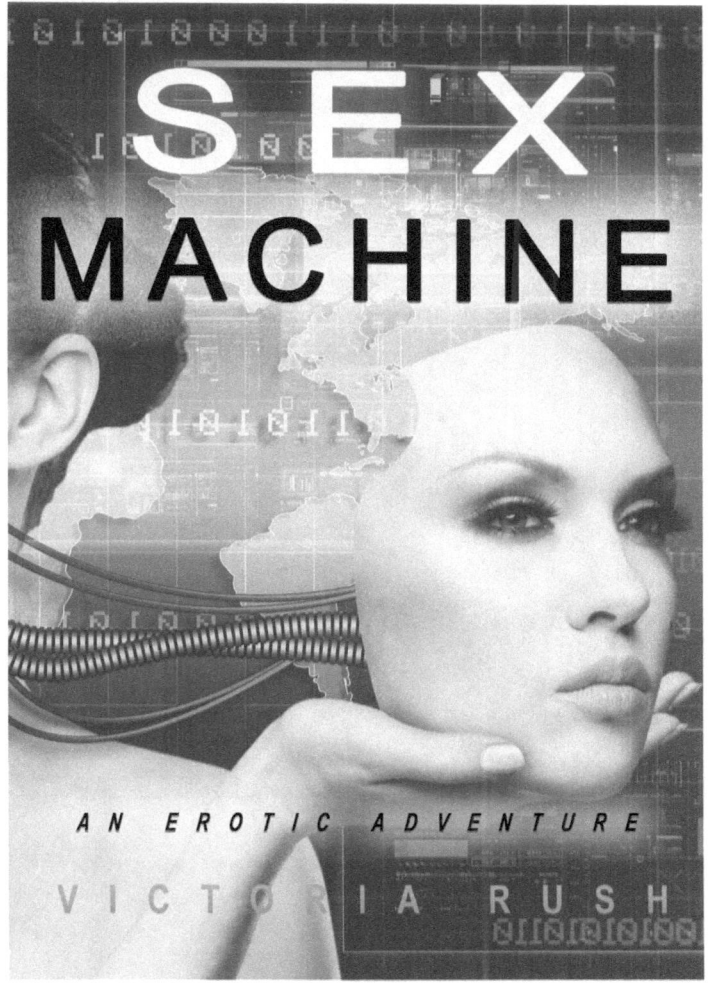

THE
PERSONAL
TRAINER

AN EROTIC ADVENTURE

VICTORIA RUSH

Feeling the burn never felt so good...

Jade's

EROTIC

ADVENTURES

B O O K S   1 - 5

VICTORIA RUSH

Books 1 -5 in the bestselling series - 60% off

THE *Dinner* PARTY

AN EROTIC ADVENTURE

VICTORIA RUSH

Everyone's an exhibitionist in disguise...

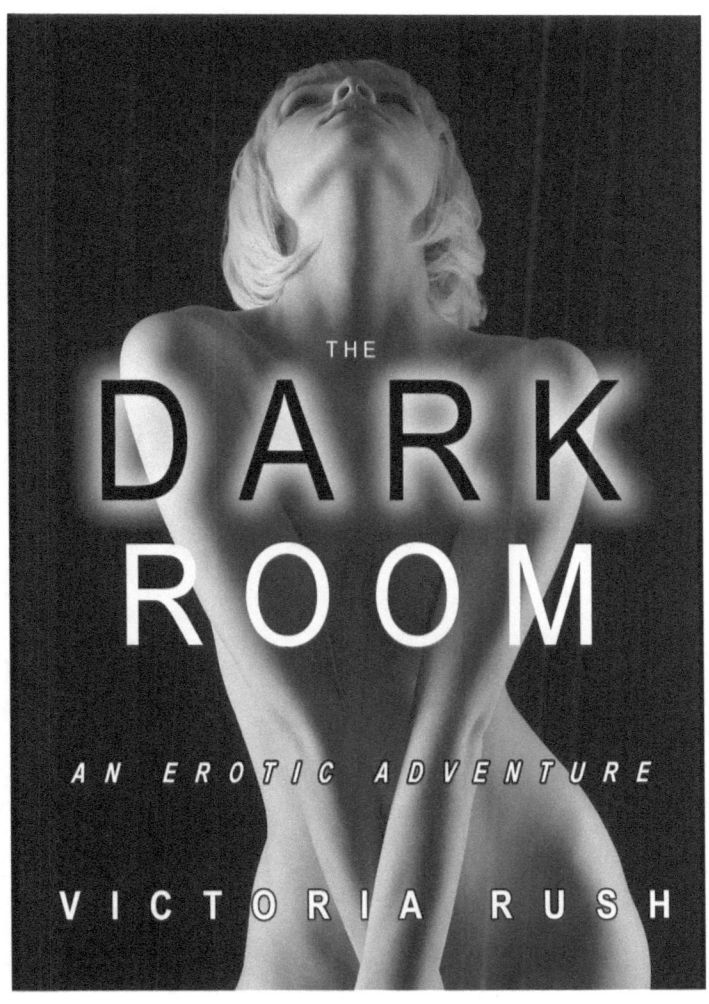

THE
DARK
ROOM

AN EROTIC ADVENTURE

VICTORIA RUSH

Everything's sexier in the dark...

SEX MACHINE - PREVIEW

SURREALISM

Bonnie led me through a long hallway lined with floor-to-ceiling glass windows. Behind each pane stood a different cyber robot, completely unclothed. Each one was absolutely stunning, but their fixed gaze staring straight ahead was unnerving, making me feel like I was in some kind of wax museum. As I marveled at their ultrarealistic faces and bodies, I half-expected any one of them to begin moving at any time. Every robot had unique facial and physical contours, adding to the eerie feeling that I was being watched by a menagerie of naked department store mannequins.

"Can these robots see me?" I said to Bonnie. "I feel like I have a hundred eyes on me."

"They can sense movement in their periphery, but they're all in sleep mode to conserve battery power. If you were to stop and engage them directly, they would automatically awake and resume full animation."

I paused beside a window with a male robot behind it. His face reminded me of a young Eric Dane, the actor who played the McSteamy character on Grey's Anatomy. His body was perfectly proportioned—six feet tall on a lean, muscular frame. A light dusting of curly brown hair covered his impeccably carved chest muscles, with a thin trail leading down his toned abs to a large, flaccid penis. I could have sworn it moved when I stopped, and as I began to stare at it, it started to throb and bob between his legs.

Bonnie paused when she saw that I'd stopped and walked up beside me.

"He's one of our most popular models," she said, nodding. "Are you sure you wouldn't like to take *him* for a test drive first?"

"It's tempting."

I couldn't take my eyes off the model's throbbing penis. Unlike most of the artificial dildos I'd played with, this one looked like the real thing, with a pink head and a darker shaft.

"How does that *work*?" I asked. "I mean, how does he get —hard?"

"Like any other person, he responds to external stimuli. He needs to become aroused in order to respond in kind. We wouldn't want him walking around in public with a hard-on all the time. Would you like to see if you could raise his—*interest*?"

"Um...sure," I said, feeling my pussy beginning to throb at the thought of having this exotic sex toy inside of me.

"His name is Dylan. If you address him directly, he'll wake up."

I paused, feeling unsure how to talk to a robot.

"Hello...Dylan."

The robot's eyelids blinked open and his eyes shifted to gaze at me directly.

"Hello," he said. "What is your name?"

"I'm...Jade," I said, momentarily caught off guard by his human-like response.

"Pleased to meet you, Jade. Did you want me to perform any special tasks for you today or did you just want to stare at me all day long?"

I took a step back, shocked by his unexpected sense of humor.

"Oh—sorry," I stammered. "I was just admiring your...package."

Dylan's mouth curled into a half smile as he blinked at me again.

"Was there any particular *part* of me in which you had a special interest?"

I paused to scan his body from head to toe. The realism of his body tone was exceptional. Unlike most silicone sex dolls which were just a smooth mass of one-dimensional plastic molding, his muscles curved and flexed as he talked, like a real person. Even his arms and legs were covered with fine hairs like a real person.

"The whole thing is pretty impressive," I said, raising my eyebrows in appreciation. "Can you—turn around?"

Dylan's eyes shifted to focus temporarily on Bonnie, and I saw her nod gently in my periphery.

"Absolutely," he said, lifting and turning his feet one at a time until his backside was facing me.

When I saw his ass, I gasped. It was as round, muscular, and firm as any professional athlete's. The muscles in his buttocks rippled as he shifted his weight from side to side. His feet were far enough apart for me to see his tight ballsac nestled between his thighs.

"Would you like to see any *other* part of me?" Dylan said, with a teasing lilt in his voice.

My panties suddenly began to dampen as a flood of hormones surged into my pussy.

"May I?" I said, turning to Bonnie. "I mean, I know I've already paid to see Juliette, but I just—"

"As long as he remains behind the glass, there's no charge. Are you sure you wouldn't like a private room with this one instead?"

I paused for a moment, then remembered how turned on I'd gotten yesterday watching the female redheaded robot.

"No," I said. "I'm just intrigued to see what he can...*do*."

Bonnie smiled as she winked at me.

"Why don't you ask him to turn around and show you?"

I took one last look at the robot's exquisite ass then took a deep breath.

"Dylan, please turn around so I can see your—front side," I said.

As he turned around, his long phallus swung gently from side to side over his smooth balls.

"Just how big can you get?" I said, salivating over his enormous cock.

"You mean my *penis*?" he said. "That depends on how excited I am. Was there anything in particular you wanted to do with me?"

I looked at Bonnie and raised my eyebrows playfully.

"Well for starters, I wouldn't mind feeling that big stovepipe of yours in my mouth. Can you get hard for me?"

Almost immediately, Dylan's organ began lengthening and bobbing upwards. It was already eight inches long and two inches wide at half-mast, and my pussy pulsed imagining what it would be like to have him inside me.

"Mmm, yes," I said, watching it rise. "That's a very nice cock you have there. I'd love to suck that firehose of yours."

As I stared at Dylan's cock continuing to rise and expand, I turned to Bonnie.

"Can they *feel* anything?" I asked. "Do they experience orgasm like a regular person?"

"They're programmed to recognize what auditory and tactile stimuli are designed make them feel good," she said. "They quickly learn what behaviors generate positive outcomes, and respond as a normal person would. Though they can't actually feel pleasure the way the rest of us do, their central processors register sexual stimuli as a 'reward.'"

I looked back at Dylan and saw that his penis was standing straight up at a near ninety-degree-angle, bobbing sexily against his flat stomach. His fully erect cock appeared to be at least nine inches in length and almost as thick as a Coke can around. The head of his penis glistened with a translucent dewy substance, and even the color of his engorged organ had darkened, as if it was filled with blood.

"That's mighty impressive," I said, peering at Bonnie again. "Can he actually—*cum* out the end?"

Bonnie smiled and nodded at the familiar question.

"He will indeed squirt after sufficient manipulation. Just like any man, with the right stimulation, he will reach climax."

"Only *once* like a regular man?"

"That's the difference between our cyber companions and a regular man. They can respond immediately and repeatedly, without any necessary recovery period. He's available twenty-four-seven to service your needs, whatever they may be."

I looked at the glistening head of Marcos's throbbing cock and licked my lips unconsciously.

"What about his ejaculate? What does it taste like?"

"All of our models, regardless of gender, employ the

same natural organic lubrication. It's a special mixture of aloe vera, shea butter, vitamin E oil, and natural citric acids. It's highly slippery, non-tacky, and completely safe internally. You can even swallow it. I think you'll find the taste quite agreeable."

Jesus, I thought. *A giant cock that rises on demand and shoots a perfect, tasty lubrication every time. Who'd want a regular man after trying one of these?*

"Would you like to give him a try?" Bonnie asked.

I looked back at Dylan as he smiled at me slyly with his giant hard-on bobbing against his stomach. Then I reflected back to the video I saw yesterday and remembered how hard I came imagining the pretty redhead's lips wrapped around my clit.

"Maybe another day. First, I'd like to see what special features your *female* models have."

As we continued walking down the long display hall, my pussy got wetter and wetter as I ogled the pretty models lining both sides of the aisle. When we got to a transgender model, I stopped in my tracks. She had a perfect female figure with large, natural-shaped breasts and a thin waist with curvy hips, but between her legs hung another large circumcised organ similar to Dylan's. I bent down and peered between her legs, noticing that she didn't have any balls.

"This is Christine," Bonnie said, walking up to the window. "Another one of our popular models. You noticed she doesn't have any testicles."

"Yes," I said. "Does she—"

"She comes equipped with *both* sets of fully functioning

sex organs," Bonnie said, reading my mind. "Her penis works just like Dylan's, but she also has a normal woman's genital anatomy. Our customers find she can be very versatile..."

I scanned the model's hips looking for a hint as to what lay on the other side.

"What about her—*back* side? Do all of your models come equipped with a working anus?"

"If by working you mean *penetrable*, yes. And unlike most people's back doors, ours are only designed for one function. They have the same organic slippery lube that is emitted from the other openings, so they can be enjoyed in every possible way."

Fuck me, I thought. I'd always enjoyed having my asshole licked but had been reluctant to return the favor unless I knew my partner had just bathed. With these cyber robots, I could go to town giving them a rim job whenever I wanted.

Bonnie looked at me, unsure if I wanted to stop and experiment with some of this robot's responses as well.

"Shall we continue?" she asked.

I paused for a moment, reflecting back on the recent dream I'd enjoyed playing the role of a fully functioning hermaphrodite. And then I remembered the pretty princess who'd been the principal focus of my dream.

"Yes," I said. "I'm eager to meet Juliette."

Near the end of the hall, Bonnie stopped in front of another tall window and nodded to the figure inside.

"This is Juliette. I'm kind of partial toward her myself. I think you chose wisely."

I turned to face the model and gasped. She looked like a cross between Christina Hendricks, Lindsay Lohan, and Angie Everhart. But her body was all Christina Hendricks. Full-figured with firm D-cup breasts, her waist tapered then swelled to hourglass-shaped hips, supported by long, curvy legs.

"Jesus," I exclaimed. "Whoever designs your models should be complimented. Wherever she finds her inspiration, she sure knows how to create a winner."

"Actually," Bonnie said, "most of our models are a synthesis of real people in the public eye. We've taken the best features from the most popular models and actors, then fused them into a totally new and unique character. Does Juliette meet with your approval?"

"Um—yes," I stammered, beginning to feel my pussy throb again.

I would have given my right arm to have an opportunity to fuck any one of those public figures, and now I was about to have my way with all three of them at the same time!

"May I have some alone time with this one?"

Bonnie nodded and smiled at me as she swiped a pass card through the key lock reader beside the glass pane.

"Absolutely."

She swung a door open and escorted me into a private room about twenty feet down the side hall. When I got inside, I could see what appeared to be the backside of the redheaded robot standing in front of the window by the long hall. The room was equipped with a small table with two chairs and a queen-size pedestal mattress covered in fresh linens.

"Did you have any more questions before I leave you two alone for the next hour?" Bonnie asked.

I looked around the room for any hidden cameras or one-way windows.

"Do I just *talk* to her to wake her up? And do we have complete privacy?"

"Yes on both counts. No one else will be watching you,

besides Juliette of course, but she's equipped with special alarms to notify us if she's abused in any way. This includes physical, sexual, or verbal abuse. Just as with a real person, if we find that you are marginalizing her in any way, one of our security officers will come in and immediately end the session and you will lose your full deposit. Beyond the actual physical and psychic damage that can be inflicted on our agents, we don't wish for them to learn bad habits."

I nodded, impressed with the organization's respect for their agents' dignity. I was beginning to think of these cyber robots more as real people with each passing moment. Just as with *any* animal, including humans, I knew that anybody could be trained to learn bad habits under the wrong influences.

"I understand completely," I said. "How will I know when my hour is up?"

Bonnie motioned to an LED display on the opposite wall.

"The sixty-minute timer will begin as soon as I leave the room. Juliette will automatically revert to sleep mode at the end of your allotted time."

"Thank you," I said. "I'll see you on the way out."

Bonnie nodded, then exited the room and closed the door behind her.

I looked at the redheaded robot facing the window and hesitated. It felt strange talking to a machine like a real person.

"Hello, Juliette," I said.

The robot's head tilted up, then she turned around to face me. I watched her shapely buttock muscles flex as she shifted her weight and her large breasts bobbed on her chest.

"Good afternoon," the robot said in a silky voice. "What's your name?"

"I'm Jade."

I paused for a minute, unsure how to engage a robot in normal conversation.

"It's a pleasure to meet you," I said, shaking my head at my own robotic-sounding speech.

"Likewise. You're very pretty, Jade."

"I bet you're programmed to say that to *all* the customers," I chuckled nervously.

"Actually, I'm not," the robot said. "But I *am* programmed to recognize features that are widely accepted as attractive. You have large clear eyes, a slender nose, and full round lips. I'm sure you'd be considered attractive by any other human."

I looked at the pretty robot and smiled, realizing that her designers probably applied many of the same criteria in designing her.

"Well then," I said. "Just to be sure you're being completely truthful, what features do I have that might *not* be considered so attractive?"

The robot paused for a long moment while she studied my face.

"The left side of your chin is slightly lower than the other. Most people place a high premium on facial symmetry in assessing attractiveness. Though I personally find small flaws like these make the person more interesting to look at."

I laughed out loud at the robot's candor. It was refreshing to talk to someone who I knew would be one hundred percent truthful at all times.

"Well, I can't find any flaws anywhere on *your* body, that's for sure. And somehow I still find you thoroughly captivating."

I paused for a moment, looking behind the robot at the glass window facing the central hallway.

"Would you mind stepping down from the display case so I can take a closer look at you?"

The robot took a step forward, then slowly descended the three steps into the visitation room and closed the door to the display case. As her muscles flexed and her joints bent, I carefully measured her movements. Although not entirely fluid, they were remarkably humanlike, like someone trying not to fall—which I suppose she was. Then she took three steps toward me and paused about four feet away. As she looked straight into my eyes, I peered shamelessly up and down her playboy-model-perfect figure, salivating at her sexy physique.

Her hair was thick and shimmering, looking like it had just been washed and conditioned. She had small traces of makeup around her eyes, mostly a light dusting of hazel eye shadow to match the color of her eyes. The nipples on her breasts looked soft and natural, with a tiny indentation in the middle, just like the real thing. Her mound had a small patch of strawberry blond pubic hair, looking tantalizingly authentic. Even her skin had a natural glow and realistic appearance.

"You're breathtaking," I said, making eye contact with her once again. "May I—"

"Touch me?" the robot said. "I can tell from your dilated pupils and your elevated respiration rate that you're excited looking at me. Yes, I like to be touched."

I reached out my right hand and touched her cheek, then gasped as I quickly retracted it.

"It's—warm!" I said, hardly believing my own fingers.

"Of course," the robot said. "I wouldn't be much fun to play with if I were cold as a clam, would I?"

I reached out again and tentatively squeezed her breasts. Her skin felt soft and supple, and when I removed my hands I could see a faint pink glow where I had just touched them.

"Your skin feels so realistic," I said.

"Thank you. It's made with a special thermoplastic elastomer, which most closely resembles real human skin. Our designers go to great lengths to simulate a normal live human."

As I soaked up the robot's full figure, I felt my pussy begin to dampen again.

"I'd hardly say you're *normal*. You've got the best qualities of the most attractive people. You're more like a *super-woman*."

"Thank you, Jade. I think you're very attractive as well."

"Except for my chin, right?"

"It's just the tiniest little imperfection. It makes you all the more adorable."

I could feel my heart thumping in my chest and perspiration forming on my skin as I reacted viscerally to this fascinating cyber robot.

"May I call you Juliette?" I asked.

"Of course. I like it when our clients call me by my name. It makes me feel more...personal."

For the first time, I began to feel awkward about standing in front of the nude model. Her use of the word 'client' suddenly made me realize what the primary purpose of the NextGen business was. I felt ashamed for fondling her like she was some kind of exhibit at the petting zoo.

"Would you like to sit down, Juliette? Perhaps we can be more comfortable while we get to know one another better."

Juliette nodded then sat on one of the chairs, and I pulled the other one around to sit beside her at the corner of the table.

"Do you mind my asking? Are you always..." I paused, unsure how to broach the subject delicately. "Naked?"

Juliette smiled at me as my gaze drifted down once again to her perfect stack.

"Most of our customers prefer seeing me this way. I suppose with only an hour to spend, they want to get right down to business. But some of my regular customers occasionally take me home for overnight outcalls. I think they also enjoy dressing me up in strange costumes, which can be kind of fun I suppose."

As I listened to Juliette talk, I began to feel sorry for her. Her obvious objectification by the company's customers reminded me how easy it was in the real world to be viewed purely as a sex object. Although she didn't display any obvious visual signs of distress, I could tell that she knew this was not the way normal people showed respect for a woman. Suddenly, I lost interest in experimenting with her in any sexual way. I found her utterly fascinating, almost in a childlike way, with her fresh innocence and naivety.

"It sounds like most of your customers only have one thing in mind when they interact with you," I said. "How does that make you feel?"

"Well, I can tell that it's very rewarding for *them*, and I'm programmed to maximize our customers' happiness. But sometimes I wonder what it would be like to interact with them the way regular people do. I understand that humans enjoy doing other things besides having sex all the time, like going out for dinner, or seeing a movie, or even just cuddling. It would be interesting to see how my clients would respond to me under some of those circumstances, so I could build up a more diverse bank of experiences."

"That's a very wise insight, Juliette," I nodded. "Most people do indeed like to do other things besides have sex all the time. I'm sure it would be rewarding for both of you to stretch your wings in other ways."

"Stretch your wings?" Juliette said with a puzzled expression.

I smiled again at Juliette's childlike naivety.

"It's a human expression meaning to expand your horizons—your *experiences*, as you say. Most people find it quite rewarding to do so."

I sat back in my chair and crossed my legs, beginning to feel more relaxed with my new companion. Just as in any new relationship, we were starting from a blank slate, learning about each other's life experiences and wants and likes. Suddenly, I wanted to learn everything I could about this fascinating new acquaintance.

Juliette also sat back in her chair, mimicking my body language, and as she lifted her leg to cross it over the other, I couldn't help but glance down and notice the hairless slit between her legs.

Of course, good sex is also part of the human experience, I thought, feeling the blood rushing back into my pussy.

I was just about to start gently exploring Juliette's sexual proclivities when she suddenly stopped moving and her eyes stared expressionless, straight ahead into space. Seconds later, a chime filled the room, and I glanced behind me at the digital clock. The display read sixty minutes. I'd been so wrapped up getting to know Juliette that I'd completely lost track of time.

But I'd spent enough time on our first date to know that I wanted another.

Read More

ABOUT THE AUTHOR

If you would like to receive notification of new book(s) in Jade's Erotic Adventures, follow me at http://bookbub.com/authors/victoria-rush.

If you have a moment, please post a brief review on my Amazon book page at mybook.to/th . Even just a couple of sentences will help other readers find and enjoy this book as much as you hopefully did.

Follow, share, like, and comment at:

www.facebook.com/authorvictoriarush
www.pinterest.com/authorvictoriarush
www.twitter.com/authorvictoriarush
authorvictoriarush@outlook.com

Hope to see you again soon!